Your Smallest Bones

Stories

SEVEN7H TANGENT

Published by Seventh Tangent in San Francisco
Edited by Laura Chapman, Kristina Kearns, and Jamie Lundy
Book Design by Sean Taylor & J. Brandon Loberg
Cover illustrations © 2014 Stephanie Thomas
Set in Baskerville Titles in Big Caslon

First Printing

Selected stories in this collection first appeared in the following:
What You're Waiting For - Instant City 8, ISSN 1937-0784,
It sings us Both to Sleep - (nominated for PushCart Prize) - Sparkle and Blink 40, ISBN 978-1-300-10313-4
Flight and Weightless - Pantheon Magazine, April 2014 ISBN 1494415577
How Josh Met Emily - Full Of Crow Quarterly, February 2014, ISSN: 2157-3530
Hands Pressing Play - Whisperings Magazine, Summer 2014, ISBN 1494415577
Where the Pickled Jalapeños Grow - Coe Review, : Volume 44, issue 2.
The Burden of Legitimacy - East Coast Literary Review, Fall Edition 2014 ISBN-10: 1500852775

ISBN 978-0-578-15298-1

for Viracocha

ALSO BY SEAN TAYLOR

Everything To Do With You

Your Smallest Bones

stories by

SEAN TAYLOR

Hey I found the safest place

to keep all our tenderness.

Keep all those bad ideas.

Keep all our hope.

It's here in the smallest bones,

the feet and the inner-ear.

It's such an enormous thing

to walk and to listen.

-John K. Samson

Contents

Flight and Weightless

"This is your opus."

At the beginning of what is now Alaska's first plain, where discoverers went to discover things (as we did) and where discoveries should have been made, before the Inuit cultures and the nose kissing, there were these strangers. And they would never say it's so damn hard to meet people in cities, but they knew it's not as easy on frozen lakes.

We tried on different hats in peculiar places: one's for fishing, one's for hunting, but they both kept our heads warm. We bought one of each and headed out to the lake.

We stood with parallel feet, two never intersecting lines, my lips on your forehead, pushing the steam to cool your hot head, which is all that was heating us before the next big push.

I wonder what's left to hurt. Is it your frozen toes?

You told me the first time you got home from the hospital that your mother had lined your coats with longhaired carpet samples.

You said, "She knew, you know?"

When I glanced down on this frozen lake I met the breath that left my lips. I tried pulling it back in, telling myself I was just steam-breathing to clear my throat, so I could tell you all those haught silly things caught like ghosts. Like how your ears will never actually hold your hair back (I'm sorry), and I can finally say for sure I'll never beat you at Boggle.

I've clipped my index finger through your belt loop and drawn our hips together. I call myself your carved-out keychain. I'm keeping you, with all your tiny and easily forgotten and endlessly important things-your tools for discovery.

We were two people, with a grand piano on thin ice. We pushed it far enough to see the ice crack like the high notes it would play. I'll push you out with it until those cold fish can enjoy the music with their cold deaf dumb ears.   We will watch them struggle and wonder how it tastes when they push their snouts to the pane, painting breath, touching face, swimming to the surface. I'm sure it's such a new and exciting air raid.

What were we doing?

I guess we were two kids playing feed the ducks in the winter, playing dance at the funeral, playing take the plane, the earthquake will soon be over.

Painkillers were holding your hand after you coughed but before you wiped your jacket.

Painkillers were the half curls in your hair, that you yourself didn't curl, that curled themselves either out of routine or out of unease.

Two years ago you were Maria and you played the piano endlessly. You stayed in Spokane and I moved to San Francisco. Your fingers were always long enough to make a point-they were your smallest bones and they were your favorites.

So we set rules. No, we set regrets. Your hair was at your shoulders and curly taut under your favorite beanie. You were a party favor smiling in winter. Maria you were half native and half unsure, and as often as the fishermen caught colds, they would say, "As long as paradise is never, then she Maria, is ever, ever, ever more." We decided if ever we were to return to each other, I to Spokane or you to San Francisco, that leaving was a mistake. Breaking up was a mistake, a foul note, my old friend the delete key. Then we would have to deal with all that time we spent apart, that buried time, and we'd be cross wondering what we did right. Then there were the butterfly effects, and forks, and cysts, and poorly timed immeasurable things.

What a terrible life like dominos, is what I had said.

When we dragged that impossible immeasurable thing out to that terrible lake neither you nor I would seem to fall over.

I was fine in San Francisco, regrets be damned. I gave you my address and said show up if you're ready to jump out of a plane. That was my promise to you, Maria-afraid-of-heights.

Come to me, admit that you're wrong to let me leave you, and jump out of a goddamn plane with me.

You can blame the mime, I'm pretty sure some people are still speechless.

I will admit I was drunk on our last night together and dreamt of you losing your old off-white beanie on our way back to earth. I heard skydiving is the most extreme way of being born again. We would leave everything's everything, and the fresh air, oh the fresh air. Some say the fall smells like a labor room, and then I wanted to take all of your favorite nurses skydiving. Then I heard it smells like what you love most because your adrenaline is cooking.

And Maria, your adrenaline smells so good.

The chalk board scratch sound of piano legs on ice is not so terrible to hear when you can measure the notes by how thick the ice is, and you can tell that less than two measures ago you were safe. So you play castanets with your frozen fingers that sound as beautiful as breaking glass. Thick spots sound like a chandelier reuniting with the ground, in the two-two timing of your favorite handclaps.

Oh Maria you were old for twenty-two. You were always spying knitting needles and staying in. Your hips worn like a veteran waitress, bouncing back and forth between staggered tables. In Spokane, in winter, you would brush your teeth with hot water, and it was disgusting.

So we pushed that piano out and made snow angels, except on the ice we called them ghost angels. Yours was called Flight and mine was called Weightless.

Two years after I said goodbye a big brown package arrived, a parachute, with your name on it. I had to sign for it; someone had to know, that I knew, it hadn't merely fallen from the sky. I opened it in my apartment, it was the size of my apartment, and in the middle of all that vinyl and rope I found a three-page note.

I pushed that piano onto that lake and your cheeks were the roses you were thrown. Your frozen hips bowed only because the cold had broken them so.

In the note you spoke of holding your own estate sale. When people asked you who had died you would just laugh, and brush your ever growing hair back behind your ears. You would cough a little, then point and raise the price of something in a fit of transference.

I remember we would go to estate sales and attempt to figure out the dying, the dead, using only what they had owned as clues. In memory, obituaries seemed to tell their tales out of respect, the way formal photographs hide scars and birthmarks. How we would brag of collecting dead grandfathers. Remember that board game Guess Who? We were trying on their winter coats, hiding in their closets like ghosts. We hoped the man who owned Venus in Furs had a hidden passage. If only we pulled the right book, perhaps something from the Marque De Sade, perhaps The story of O? We bought their old war periscopes, we lied and called them our family heirlooms. We dreamt them left to us with maps and keys. We were the children of sailors, pirates, and butchers.

Your note said that people only bargain at estate sales when the dead aren't in the room. They will, however, sneer as if you're leaving the country with their currency, as if the price of this jewelry box should be lower because heaven knows you won't need it where you're going.

When we pushed that piano out I knew you played much better without gloves or mittens or cancer too. You were once the little girl in church running loose with a bed of hair upon your head tied in ways only mothers knew, wearing those horrible PTA sweaters adorned with oversized treble clefs.

You said I had to come back and make my regret, I had to break a promise or two.

You were diagnosed cold, in a stale white room. You said it smelled of bleach and peanut butter, and you said you were so sure of it. I packed up the parachute, the note, and some endless amount of jackets.

· · · ·

Now you can imagine me with a carry-on parachute on a commercial airliner, promising everyone, "I won't be opening it, it's really all I have to have."

On an airplane they will not believe you when you say a parachute is all you have to have.

I guess you took all the money you earned from that estate sale and bought this parachute, and it was two thousand dollars on sale.

You bought a parachute on clearance.

I laughed, a dying girl blows her life savings on a parachute, how cliché.

So I sold all I owned and bought a plane ticket.

It was the last available seat on the worst airline they had available. I bought it with the insurance of my own parachute.

By the time we got that grand piano to the middle of the frozen lake we shook hands in mitts so quickly I'd thought we'd start a fire in friction. I was afraid of falling into the lake like I was afraid of being hit by a train, or skydiving, or of dial tones, and other serious life-ending things.

On the flight to Spokane I hugged the parachute like I was holding you.

To the frightened flight attendant I could not stress enough, this is not a bomb… this saves lives. Besides she was only doing her job working for a terribly complicated machine she will never understand. She was, after all, an American.

They knew there was ice on the runway and they cut off our drinks as soon as we began the landing procedure. I had never flown before and those busy flight attendants strapped next to their TV dinners and mini-bar liquor kits just seemed to smile so nervously. I've seen those faces before. I once saw a National Geographic about the people who survived from being stranded on desert islands. They spent the rest of their lives playing the same saved face to every over flying plane. I'd figured by the end of the program that these survivors would have all the answers too. They didn't. Worst of all they didn't even start up the show with "If you were trapped on a desert island..."

These people stranded on desert islands dreamed of the same planes that flew the people stranded on crashing planes dreaming of desert islands.

Sure enough when the turbulence started everyone looked at me as if to say, "Why didn't I think to bring a parachute?"

Even the flight attendant, I can see it in her eyes, she thinks it for a living.

The captain slides and kicks the plane like a filthy pig in frozen mud, his only two feet jabbing at the darkness below his swollen belly at those numerous pedals. Everyone on board claps as we land, though I remember the in-flight film ended hours ago.

"Welcome to Washington."

Laughing like the veins on our foreheads.

I am home.

I throw the pack on my back with my extra jackets and run straight for the exit terminal, still having never sky-dived despite my best efforts not to. Congratulations Maria I am still without regrets.

When I've reached your doorstep with my tire-chained-Alamo-escorted-Chevy-Aveo, your house doesn't have a quarantined circus tent, ET doesn't even live here. When you answer the door you aren't all nose-tubed for oxygen, you aren't in a bed with those tie-down steel rails, you aren't even limping. You're just eyes and lips and ready for everything, still all bones and movement, still wearing no shoes in the snow, all Maria with your hair down, this time to your elbows.

"What do we do now?" I asked you, parachute on my back, spinning the rental car keys around my fingerless gloves with the same grace as anyone wearing about ten layers of California clothing, about ten layers not enough.

You say you don't know, and smile as much as you're allowed. You skip through the snow to the rental car, open the door, and sit down.

While I drive you aimlessly around I'm staring at all the drivers and passengers we pass by, mostly soccer practice in the snow, mostly Christmas shopping. I try so hard to give them a more difficult deed than the one I have in my passenger seat.

You say you're hungry but don't know where to eat. You say the lake is frozen but only two feet. You say San Francisco must be beautiful compared to this and apologize frequently. I head straight to the worst and slowest stoplight in town and wait.

Right before it turns green I lean over and give you the worst kiss I have ever. It's all teeth and bones like preteens, k,i,s,s,i,n,g, and then the light goes green.

"Where's the piano?" I asked kicking the front tires in the snow.

"Behind the high school. I've tenured the Make a Wish Foundation" you laugh.

You aren't supposed to be good at this.

You're supposed to be all awkward and ill and tired. Maybe you're moderately deranged, or awfully offended by how terribly I kissed you. Maria your hair's supposed to be shorter, falling out, falling apart.

I'm straight to the railroad tracks off Fifteenth Street. You used to take me here. Standing on the tracks we would count down the first thirty-seconds, and then kiss the second thirty knowing full and well the train would hit us if we stayed for the whole minute.

You told me this is how we ration; we have thirty-seconds before impact, thirty-seconds to forget everything.

We had some close calls as most all teenagers do, and we always said while we were walking away, "If you loved me like a French film we would both be dead."

Here we are and you are so cloudy confused it isn't until I start counting down from thirty that you realize I'm wearing a watch. I'm wearing a wire. We can kiss or you can laugh but I'm hoping we can still just be children playing with death. Instead it's just one tear after another and I yell, "GO," at five-seconds, and find out you won't be carried, you must be thrown.

BackintotheChevyAveo.

I throw a scarf around your neck and wrap your face so fast I call you a ninja. You call me the new light speed champion. You tell me now that I've saved your life I can finally take it. I don't know what to say so you call me a stupid head, then you tell me it isn't in your brain.

. . . .

We're off to our favorite park in winter, the frozen grass cracks under our feet and there are no geese to feed so we will eat the bread we brought. The sun sets sometime we're unsure of, the clouds are just playing that game. I give you all the jackets that I brought and am not currently wearing. You shine them on and wear them like surrender blankets on your shoulders, never in your arms.

Aren't you supposed to need these things?

Every time the park patrol rolls by we hide, lying flat on our backs. I get to hold your hand and freeze my ass off and exhale and pretend that I can breathe when the wind stings my lips. The long white frozen tips of the grass reflect brightly off of their flashlights, it's blindingly beautiful, just enough to hide me, to hide us. Still they push their flashlights across us like a Sonogram, like a CAT scan, all bright white waiting for a dip in the radar.

You roll over and kiss me and tell me, "We can be the illegal growths of this park. We can hide beneath the radar waves, and we can kick and roll our arms and make cement handshakes and snow angels."

Then with your excitement up in flames he sees us, and we're off running fast. We're burning coal and spewing breath and when we're safe, we're safe behind that dumpster behind that strip mall, and you tell me it isn't in your lungs.

I wonder if this isn't an elaborate hoax.

When do the goddamn fireworks begin?

Who coined winter wonderland? Were they not aware of hypothermia and giving up, and goddamn Spokane?

I swear Maria, I can aside, and I will.

I've never been to a funeral. I've never helped someone die. I am the blind child running up and down the pews, smelling the oak and listening to the bells.

Where are your bells? Your red flags?

We're all just showing ribs when we're weak, and I can almost count your... thirteen? It's a shaky destiny.

On our way back to my single room at the Double Tree we pass healthcare billboards asking us about "The Essentials to Health" to which you respond with a delicate snore. I'll help you to my door and this is where you can and will pass out. I ask you what your parents might think and you tell me, "If you had X days left how would you spend them?"

I tell you, "Maria I would care less."

"Good, you see what I mean."

I ask about your diet as we lay on the bed eating all the candy bars from the mini bar and then surgically replacing them with items around the room in their body bag wrappers. We put the toilet paper core in the Snickers wrapper, the toothbrush in the Toblerone, and filled the little gin with a little mouthwash and seal the plastic with heat and steady hands.

"How would you eat?" Is your response, "How would you live?"

"Yeah but I'm not the one who's…"

"Who's what?"

"Never mind," I roll over and wrestle some pillows.

You kill the lights and I can feel the bed creak and warm as you shuffle close to me. Then you breathe into my left ear, first breathing light as if to say listen to me, then heavy like please stay asleep, don't talk back, just keep listening.

I am awake and listening.

You tell me the doctor told you there will come a day when you will wake up and will have forgotten which hand you write with.

You tell me your mother sewed small pillows into the knee caps of your jeans just in case you took up prayer. She knew your skin was weak and would break so much easier.

I remember when you used to stay up all night dripping wax between the keys of your piano, saying your fingers needed to be stronger, your favorite little bones. I asked if you would ever sleep, and you would say you would when you were dead.

"Maria…" I whisper, "Where is it?"

. . . .

I woke up to you underlining numbers in the Gideon Bible and then ever so carefully, without causing a crease in the spine, taping a hundred dollar bill to a certain page, then replacing it in the bedside table drawer.

You were either leaving a treasure hunt via some insane mathematical equation for the next devotee, or simply underlining all mentions of the devil and greed. Then taping the bill to page six hundred and sixty-six.

Someone, somewhere, will someday, never know you, and know this.

It's easy to assume, and figure, it figures.

I roll over and scratch your back asking if you've given god any thought. It feels a little as if I'm just cheating on your exam, prepping myself for this awful experience I have no experience with.

"No, why would I?"

"Its Sunday…"

"There was a one-in-seven chance. When do you fly back?"

I sit up and find the back of your neck with my lips, marching them up and down the arch between the two straps of your beautiful, tired, pink slip, which I'm pretty sure looks dated back to the 1920s.

"Good morning to you as well. I haven't bought a ticket. I was thinking of taking the train."

You don't hear me, maybe you do. You just turn around, and fall back into bed.

"Where did you get this thing?" I ask as I tug at the borders of lace that frame you.

"An estate sale."

With that I've forgotten that we're not two years ago. We're not waiting out another winter. We're not sleeping in until the sun saves us. You encourage my crooning kisses and lean back into me. I tell you (like they do in the movies), "Everything will be all right."

You're back brushing your teeth with hot water and you bite off the hair of your toothbrush, to find your subtle strength. It was everywhere, you said, "And it's all mine," foaming at the mouth with paste. You're laughing too loud to finish your own joke. You were fighting cancer, one wrecking ball gasp at a time, still strong enough to make your own knees weak.

You asked me why my lips were so torn up, "Have you been biting them? Who's been biting them? Is it the cold?"

You're worried, like you're worried, and I like it. Once again you're late and just in time.

"It just feels right here, in Spokane. I think I'm biting them because you aren't."

Then you hit me because I won't hit you back.

Then I run outside and I've warmed up the car and I joke about it. It's not because you're dying, it's because I'm a gentleman. So you hit me again to make sure, and I kiss you to finalize it.

Our first stop today is the U-haul lot where we convince a man this steer of a Chevy Aveo (a subcompact economy pushcart) can pull a trailer with a full size piano in it through fresh snow. I feel foolish, and I know it's probably not going to work. So I talk up the tire chains and the torque and catch him winking at you just before he says all right.

All right, all right…

I know now, everyone knows, Spokane knows, you're dying, and I try hard not to obviously swallow hard.

I take the keys from the clean counter top and lock up the unstable, unsafe trailer. When you see the brake lights communicate with my right foot, you're so beautifully thumbs-up through the frost bitten window. You run back into the passenger seat and press your long fingers into the grated heater vents, turn and smile, "Ready?"

"Ready as ice to melt."

Stoplights this time around mean I'm looking up various definitions of "Assisted Suicide," on Wordbook, on Wikipedia, on an IPhone. My cracked cold brick fingers are bone sticks, they're locked. They're blindly jabbing flesh daggers, darting like I'm spear fishing on a touch screen. I laugh blindly, sluggishly, remembering and placating my old friend the delete key.

"Assisted suicide is the process by which an individual, who may otherwise be incapable, is provided with the means [drugs or equipment] to commit suicide."

When we pushed that piano out on that frozen lake the dents and dimples in the ice shook and fought the key's hammers into tickling the strings. This brought it to play like a small-time Richter scale, measuring the punching suspension and depth with sound; and we laughed like metal detectors in a minefield. So we pushed it carefully, and I remember when we used to play that board game "Operation" with numb hands, except we called it Eskimo Doctors.

"Suicide facilitated by another person, esp. a physician, who organizes the logistics of the suicide, as by providing the necessary quantities of a poison."

We dragged that black piano out like a casket to the white ice of the frozen lake, like the top of our wedding cake.

While I was away, before you played calendars like chess games, you practiced all of your favorite artists' last works. I remember on the way to the lake that day listening to

Beethoven's fifteenth, Holy song of thanks, and Mozart's deaf Requiem.

"But what are you closing with?" I ask as you shuffle through your latest mix tape while we pass by a church that just let out. The partitioners are all penguins in big black and grey coats, they all seem to start to gossip about a runaway piano, a real tear jerking symphony. I can tell that they're talking about us. We have to slow down because they're mostly old, and the road is slick black ice. I had to lay on the horn to break their idle chitchat, to change their subjects, and I don't miss home that much anyway.

"I've been writing since you left, I have a couple compositions, I had to have some."

"Are they recorded? Can I listen to them, all wrapped up in my new parachute?"

"HEY! That parachute is for jumping first."

I get it Maria, you're smarter than I knew; you're making your regret come true too. Everything you owned, everything you ever were, everything was sold, liquefied into a parachute. So when I jump you're jumping with me.

"I get it." I want to say cop out, and, or, cheater but you're doing the best that you can do.

"But yeah I made a tape" you pat your red coat pocket. "It's all that's left."

"Is it any good?"

You respond with a couple slugs to my arm, and I laugh, and you point to the road.

After I pushed that grand piano into the middle of that Lake I stood up all mittens and pea coat, yelling, "I grant you Exodus!"

I backed it up into a tree, into a rock, and I think under that patch of snow over there was a creek. I was delaying the inevitable and endlessly inexperienced. I wonder if the U-haul guy was okay with the rental because he knew we would fail. Those hairy thick forearms resting on the counter like the countless logs in our path. We kept circling the lake looking for hidden paths, and when I found your favorite my hands finally begin to shake. Luckily the cold already had my nose running and red.

"You okay?" you ask as I catch my breath just a tiny bit too violently.

"Yeah this cold just kills my sinuses…"

Kills, yeah, it kills them.

You're so strong, pointing me with mittens in tow, getting out and guiding me with those thumbs up and come hither signs. Then comes the all feared two palms up, the stop, and then the wave me out, the "here we are," and the "let's do this."

I drop the gate to the trailer, and it comes crashing down loud enough to scare away half the birds on the lake.

"I thought they knew you were coming. Where are they going? You told me this was a sold-out show…" I say to you.

"Comeonletsdothis," you say.

"Huh?"

"I said come on, help it down the ramp, the legs will break if we're not careful."

"We don't have to do this," I plea.

"Yes, we do. You promised. I said I would sky dive, and you said you would help me play on a frozen lake, on this frozen lake."

"You're right. How far are we going?" My voice trails off because I don't want you to hear me, because I don't want you to say what you're about to say next.

"To the middle, to the very middle, where the fish can hear me best, where the ice is as thin and tired as I am, to the middle." But you still said it, and you said it with every word louder than the last, because you wanted me to hear you, so that I would say this next.

"Get the left side, the hammers and strings are heavier on the right, watch out for that root by your right foot."

Down the ramp we lost the wheels off two of the legs. We lost the second two due to weight leverage issues on the ice, and they cracked popped like stomping on Christmas lights.

When we got to the middle we were tiptoeing with a grand piano like a pair of professional circus thieves, the legs now sharpened from the spinning slide across like ice skates.

"What if you play it and it doesn't fall in?"

"I don't want to die in a hospital."

"What if you played it and it fell in but you got away?"

"I don't want to die in a hospital, it smells like bleach and peanut butter."

"We could go back to San Francisco and jump out of airplanes until it kills us. We could be born again, and again, and again, until we got it right."

I can tell you I'm not afraid of jumping out of planes. I'm not afraid of getting hit by trains. Right now I am scared of frozen lakes, and of cancer.

I ask for the tape and you give it to me and I start to walk away.

"Wait, Maria... Where is it?"

"It's in my bones." And finally your voice breaks.

I walk far enough away to consider myself safe. Then I walk ten feet farther and lie down and remake my ice angel, "Weightless."

"This is my resignation to a frozen lake. What did you do over winter break?" I say to myself.

It must be two o'clock because the sun is so high and the town is so quiet.

You told your few favorite friends to listen in at two. I wonder if they're poaching the woods, and where they're poking out their heads. Or how they see me in this situation. The ex-boyfriend lying cold on his back. The ex-boyfriend that came to send you away because all the other boys ran when they saw your blood work.

Oh Maria, how your blood does work.

You start playing so I close my eyes, and I can feel it, I can feel you, just like you wanted me to. It's turning in my back as much as it is in my ears. It's beautiful and I wish you could feel it like I do.

Maria on ice, you're so cold.

I turn my head and you're playing like an Eskimo wedding. With your favorite tiny dying bones, and your hair down to your lower back. Your fingers lifting fancifully, and then falling back down like guillotines. It is priceless, and I regret leaving you, I regret not making more of you with you. I regret running away with an endless breadcrumb black cape, and the teasing, and the games.

You just made my regrets, our regrets, and your regrets are now everyone's regrets. It's graceful, like dominos, we all fall in love, with all these regrets. I'm left prize-fighting my way across the ice, clumsy with no piano anchor, and no steady Maria. I hope her friends see me too, and I hope they're laughing.

I give up again. I've fallen down, and I'm ear to the ground. I'm frostbitten and if my heart could slow down I would tell you this.

You aren't (despite your best efforts) left.

I'm going to listen until you fall in, and even then you haven't passed away. You've preserved in me, and I'm staying alive, parachute in hand. I'm an escape artist dying to stay.

With my ear to the Lake I can hear your toe tapping, and the vanilla C sharp, and the deep chocolate E. I can see my breath pushing faster to the beat. I try to lift up but my ear is stuck. I'll wait through spring and buy the lake house on the North end. I'll play your tape every Friday night to the fish.

And you won't die in a hospital.

And when you forget to remember what we always did, we discovered Alaska's first plain. We pushed our noses together, and made the mistake of meeting on frozen lakes, born clumsy and died the same.

How Josh Met Emily

He feared growing up to be the kind of man that would invent the back scratcher, to be that kind of alone.

It seemed as if the rain came down all day in fifteen-minute increments every thirty minutes. Josh stood at the window of his third-floor apartment on Haight Street with an old stopwatch his grandfather left him, and he watched. He watched dark and light clouds come in from the West, and the rain they carried with them. He watched and he waited for the umbrellas of the passer-by to bloom. When the umbrellas opened he started the stopwatch, and when they closed he stopped it. He pressed his weight into the glass of the window with his left shoulder and forehead, not at all concerned that should the glass break, his fall would be fatal.

At two o'clock, after two hours of these timed measurements of precipitation, he gave up and went out. He estimated that his journey west, into the storm, into Golden Gate Park, would take roughly half an hour walking, or ten minutes on his bike. These estimates were made with a thread of string against an old map-it matched the length of the legend's measured mile. The string was yanked from an old sock, abandoned due to the liability of its holes, one on the heel, the other small and thinning on the corner of the smallest toe.

He used the once-sock-string to measure the distance between his apartment and the Japanese Tea Garden. It was slightly over one mile away.

Sure enough once outside his door the umbrellas of fellow commuters shot up and out in a burst of resistance. Josh, with less than the budget of an umbrella owner, simply threw his hood over his crestfallen head and pushed forward. The pedestrian traffic seemed minimal as he walked up Haight Street, and he wondered how many other onlookers spied dry spells from bay windows for optimal travel times. How many others would give up and go out in the end, succumbing to such inconveniences?

His coat was large, brown, and in the style of a longshoreman or a military dock hand. It ended just above his knees and collected a number of cargo pockets which he left mostly empty. He enjoyed the anonymity and warmth of it, its blanketed fashion not in the least aesthetically pleasing. Once into the park he placed his headphones into his ears and set his Music player to shuffle the entirety of his music catalog.

On his walk he listened to Simon and Garfunkel's The Sound of Silence twice back-to-back merely by chance. The first instance of the song was supplied by their Greatest Hits album, the second coming from the soundtrack to one of his favorite films, The Graduate. He originally took this as some sort of an

omen-as random chance is often mistakenly taken. The fact that
out of some three thousand songs on his music player the only
repeat possible should strike him here, now, on a rainy day like
today, left him questioning more than it should have. He did
listen to the encore in it's entirely, and then silently thanked his
player for the beautiful coincidence by sliding his thumb across
the screen, ensuring it stayed dry.

To his surprise, after paying the entrance fee, Josh found the
Tea Garden nearly free of tourists. He approached the still scene
with a hesitancy, peering around the tall deep green manicured
topiary, assuming behind something, anything, hoards of loud
obnoxious sightseers would be perched. Yet again, and again,
they were not. Throughout his five years in San Francisco he
never knew the Japanese Tea garden to be serene, or peaceful, or
meditative, as he always dreamed it would be.

The tea garden was in theory his heaven from everyone. He
fully embraced the koi ponds' quiet harmony, or the delicate lines
combed into the sand gardens. He always wanted to rake that
sand until it was his, his millions upon millions of tiny rocks, his
galaxy aligned.

He took a seat facing the small creek after ordering a pot of
green tea and some almond cookies from the cafe. He placed his
standing order number outside of his view, raised his head to the
sky, and closed his eyes. Last night in his sleep he found a dream
of this place. He decided after waking, regardless of weather, he

would follow that dream. He would recreate it to the best of his ability, as a day hobby. In the dream he found himself alone somewhere he only knew people to be, and it was quiet, except for the rain. The rain fell to find gutters, ledges and rooftops in the off timing to the percussion track of every storm. Josh closed his eyes and waited for it all to steady in peace, as it did in his dream.

"What's your name?" She asked him first. Her question came flooding in from his dry shower. His eyes opened to a small girl, with straight black hair and small black eyes. She looked to him no older than nine or ten. She was dressed in a long thick white coat that came down past her knees to her ankles, where large white boots shot back up her legs. She was kept covered, nearly completely, save her tiny hands and her face.

"Josh, my name is Josh. What's yours?"

"My name is Emily... What are you doing?"

"I'm listening to the rain, shh, can you hear that?" he said, hoping to either bore or occupy her. Both would keep her subdued, either would do just fine. "Close your eyes and look up. Breathe in the rain. Smell it and just listen."

She did as he asked, mostly, kind of, she only peeked at him a little from the corner of her eye. After two long breaths she exclaimed, "I don't like to close my eyes, it's too dark. I don't like to sleep, either."

What he said next he did not think to say.

"Well, you know you should get used to it. After this life is over that's all there is, just closed eyes and the sound of rain."

He caught himself off guard after saying that. She was a child, regardless of his poor mood, Simon and Garfunkel, or the weather. He put his hand over his mouth and touched his lips as if expecting pain from making such a crude statement. Nonetheless she responded cool as ever.

"How do you know?" she asked.

"I don't, I just figure."

"Well, I thought after life you go to Heaven. My mom says in Heaven your shoes never get untied. My shoes are always getting untied, that's why I have to wear boots, I just slip them on."

"Well, what if I just like the sound of rain with my eyes closed? Can that be my Heaven?"

The tea arrived, and after the waitress disappeared Josh added about two ounces of cheap brandy from an aluminum flask he pulled out of the very large breast pocket of his coat.

Emily watched him add the brandy without flinching. She seemed to think less than anything of it however, as if he were merely adding sugar or cream to his coffee.

"I guess so," she continued, "I mean, if you liked the sound of rain so much with your eyes closed, wouldn't you never get anything else done? Why not just go to Heaven now then?"

Josh soon became concerned, he felt trifled with even. With no idea where this girl's parents were he felt chosen to babysit the obligation of staying alive, as it is now embodied in a small girl named Emily.

He took a large pull at his tea, then broke one of the almond cookies in half, and presented it to her. Glancing down he noticed it was nearly the size of her entire hand. She accepted the cookie. She ate it much like the squirrels across the path did, with both hands close to her mouth, nibbling around the almond in the center. Josh saw this as an opportunity to tell Emily exactly what was going to happen if you go to Heaven of your own accord.

"You see, if you go to Heaven on purpose..." He started and stopped, endlessly careful with each word. He listened to them as if they were being told to him by a wiser, older Josh. "You don't get to go to Heaven. Its like the eleventh commandment or something. You go to a place that's the opposite of Heaven, where your shoes are always untied."

He swallowed the vacuum these words leaving left, the great absence they created asking him suddenly to breathe. Emily, unfaltering, just kept on.

"My mom also says that in Heaven your hair stays the perfect length and you never have to cut it, it is always perfect."

"Well, in opposite Heaven every time you make scrambled eggs the shells break into a million pieces, then you spend eternity picking them out of the yolk."

Josh gave up. He was on a one-way train to his truth. I'm sorry Emily, he thought, but you started this. He coughed slightly, and then took two more strong pulls at his brandy tea.

"I bet in Heaven when you trim your fingernails they always tear just right across, they never bleed."

"Well, in opposite heaven your socks are always inside-out, no matter what, and forever wet around the collar."

"In heaven you never get a runny nose because everything smells so good. It smells like flowers, not like stupid rain."

Emily was becoming fussy, Josh could sense it. Josh was already fussy, and Emily knew it.

"Oh yeah. In opposite Heaven when you put on a belt it never fits right, one hole is too tight, and the next hole is way too loose."

"Nobody wears belts in real Heaven, 'cause they don't wear pants."

"They don't wear pants?" Josh asked.

"No, they wear robes. Haven't you seen the pictures?"

Emily was right, she knew she was right. Josh knew she was right too.

"Emily, get over here, your brother is sick, we have to go home," a woman's voice called from behind them both. Emily spun lightly at the sound of her mother's voice, and in doing so dropped what was left of the cookie. Josh raised his head to the reprieve of this woman's voice, no longer looking down on Emily.

"I have to go now, goodbye." Emily said quickly. She would have said, "Have a nice day," had it yet been introduced int"o her vocabulary, but it wasn't, so she didn't.

"Goodbye."

Hands Pressing Play

When she hits the nail on the head, she builds a house. She gathers up all of her possessions, and she moves in.

"I lost my job."

Sara requested they sit outside, she said it was because of the weather. She didn't necessarily lie, by telling the truth. She knew that she'd be biting at her fingernails nervously throughout their meeting, a behavior that is typically frowned upon indoors. She knew she would be all news and teeth. She wore thin silver rings she spun with her thumb on nearly every other finger. The feeling of them touching, rubbing, grinding, or the possibility of the feeling, sickened her. During her years as an accountant, Sara became unusually attentive to these unusually small things, the zipper of her sweatshirt needing to come to meet the zipper of her jeans, splitting her symmetrically. She needed it, for comfort, much like her spinning rings.

"So what's your plan then?" Colleen asked, attempting to slow Sara down.

"Well, do you want the good news or the bad news?" Sara countered.

Colleen just waited.

"I got approved for unemployment this morning ... and I have rent but not enough for my place. So I'm moving out ... my old apartment is half packed and loaded into the back of my car," she pointed up the street, "all of only the necessities, of course. And ... as for my new apartment, I got a room at the hotel."

"You got a room at the hotel? Thee hotel? My hotel? The Alphabet Hotel? Wait, what was the good news, and what was the bad news?"

"Yep, same floor even, apartment K, I'll be just down the hall from you. It's all just new news, kind of just lots of new news..."

Sara had always criticized Colleen for living in a hotel, even though it was strictly a "rent by the week" hotel.

Now since losing her job she too would have to make the sacrifice of splitting her address with twenty-five other letters. The building was perfect in that symmetry, four floors with six rooms each. Colleen claimed the "Y" and "Z" were kept quiet in the basement. The building started with "A" on the top floor and down the hall, ultimately leaving "V" closest to the front door. Each floor shared a kitchen and two communal bathrooms, one bathroom with a shower and toilet, one with a bath and toilet. The bathrooms were adjacent and centered on each floor and the plumbing ran straight up the building on both sides for each.

The kitchens were also toward the center, across from the only indoor staircase, as well as an old and noisy elevator. Every twenty years or so the building saw basic renovations, but always managed to retain its low-income fashion with a specific sort of tenant. Everyone was either artist-hoping-to-make-it poor or not-willing-to-work-more-than-a-day-a-week poor. The landlord placed Colleen in the artist category and Sara in the work-one-day-a-week category.

Colleen was an artist, though she never mentioned it in her rental application. It showed in a million tiny ways, like her confusion between colored pencils and eyeliner, or the needles that hung from her hems. She was applying to the Art Institute downtown and hoping to be accepted for the fall semester. Sara lost her job with an accounting firm after the tax season, which would not have been surprising if it were in her first year with them, but it wasn't, it was her third. They met every Sunday night at the cafe across the street from the Alphabet Hotel to catch up, they usually spoke of advancing male co-worker glances, Colleen's estranged art ideas, or Sara's weekly workload.

"After dinner, I'll help you unpack," Colleen offered.

"Thanks, the sooner I get that car unloaded the sooner I can load it back up with all of my not so necessities. I was thinking about having a garage sale except I don't have a garage? So instead do you think I could just fake an estate sale ... Would that be tacky? I know a good chunk of me is dying with that apartment. So it wouldn't be a complete lie."

After finishing their wine Sara paid the bill in thanks for the offered help and they moved slowly down the block to her packed car. Once there, Sara threw her arms to the sky and announced herself too intoxicated to drive. "Ah-ha," yelled Colleen, "I have an idea." She sprinted into a nearby grocery store parking lot and temporarily abducted a shopping cart. "Load her up!" she ordered. It took them three shopping cart trips to empty her car into apartment K.

After their exhausted goodbyes Colleen headed up to Room G and Sara back to her old apartment. There, Sara opened another bottle of wine and found herself drunkenly knocking her books down from her bookshelf. Tipping them by the tops of their spines and kicking a cardboard box below to catch them. She made jokes as they fell, she said things like, "Dictionary down!" and "Western Art History coming in for a landing." She was old enough to be doing this, she was still young enough to be drunk.

"Sara is eight for ten tonight, let's see if she can put this one away ... it's at the buzzer ..." and with that a very old and heavy copy of Shakespeare's Collected Works came crashing down and due to its sheer size missed her cardboard collection box. She overshot it entirely. The book landed splayed wide open as if in pain, the bang on her hardwood floor jolting her a little sober, mostly just more awake. While bending over to pick up the book, about ten pages fell out of the back. "Aw, come on," She said to herself and began to feed them randomly thirty pages or so into the front. These found fallen pages were smaller than those of the books, and made of thicker paper. They did blend themselves, color-wise, with the book, wearing the same yellowish brown allocated to most relic documents. While feeding them back into the book she noticed that they were blank, then on her way to the trash bag to throw them away she noticed they were not. They were covered in the goose bumps of braille, and there were not ten of them but eight.

With this she headed straight for the wine left on her makeshift nightstand of an upturned packing box beside her twin sized bed. Once there she studied these brilliant braille bumps with a few unexpected jolting hiccups. She surmised that the fallen pages must be one page letters. They were comprised of a small grouping of bumps in the top left corner, about two medium sized paragraph herds in the middle, then marking their exit with one or two short lines towards the bottom. Sara in her newly regaled hopelessly hopeful state, with her rest wine-assured, laid back into her bed and closed her eyes.

She began to run her fingers across the letters on the letters-across the bumps. The perfect penmanship of braille comforted her. She found comfort in knowing the letter had been proofread this way, with only fingers, then once received read again this way. She wondered how many fingers had passed over these papers, and felt their typed punched bruises. She wanted to read them. Were they addressed business or pleasure? To family, friend or colleague? She relayed their travel as if they were tourists, asking the lost questions of a stranger. The infinite demands of her questions collusions leaving her in a sense more tired than past passed out, and so helplessly she slept.

Sara woke up the following Monday unemployed for the ninth day that month. She learned to jump by pulling her pants up, her skin tight jeans, legs spring loaded from falling into the day. She put off packing the last of her life and headed to the library, where she checked out a book titled, "The History and Translation of Braille." It was hardbound and plain, a rose red cover with the weight and build of an encyclopedia. The book was translated throughout, the cover, the copyright page, each and every letter held out below it a collection of bumps, shadowed by its own upraised pock marks.

She then returned to her old apartment and packed up the last of her "absolute must haves," except her mattress. She placed everything she had planned to sell or throw away upon her mattress, and before turning out the light she looked upon this island she had created. She would not be able to rescue her mattress until all of the items were gone. It was her lifeboat, and it was currently drowning.

Apartment K, however, was concurrently a bomb shelter for Sara's well being. Small and nearly stuffed, a purveyed model of her perfected minimalism.

All of her lasting possessions were pushed, stacked up, lining the walls, and she felt surrounded by only herself. She decided before hoping to find sleep on a collection of blankets and pillows, on this, the first night in her new life, that she would translate what seemed to be the shortest of her found documents, the braille pages. The translation was only difficult at first because she made it so. Both her excitement and finding the first couple of words kept her from simply writing each letter above its corresponding set of raised bumps. This would have completed her task in only twenty-six semi strenuous steps. She realized this only after completing the first sentence. It read, "I marched today without you through all of the spiderwebs of Russia."

The translation in whole below:

My Lillith,

I marched today without you through all of the spiderwebs of Russia. Can you feel them now? At first, I thought I must be lost in your hair, I played my hands through them, separating them. I plucked them when they ran a bridge across my open mouth I played the vibrations over my lips. Can you hear them yet? They sound like you. As I pushed farther forward this web tangled ran round my ears, they came to split my hair with theirs. I walked far enough into them that I could not see myself to be without you. I still wear them somewhere as I sit here, and when I shower I do not clean of you, and if I do, I return to all of the spiderwebs of Russia. I go to gather your hair and you and leave it always somewhere. When I leave full of you I am heavier than when I came, and I move slowly throughout my day, all of your hair wearing the cold wind better than I do. Can you feel them yet?

I cannot come home. I have taken to cleaning out some old factories, for which I do not know what was manufactured inside. I hope the enclosed cheque helps you through this month. As soon as they keep me from work, I will no longer be kept from you. I learned something today, wind moves horizontally, while a draft moves vertically. Did you know that? I think, this life, it needs to move through your body, like a draft, it needs to play us like the air though an instrument. Can you feel it now?

Your love, Henry.

While traversing the alphabet hotel's thin hallways Sara spread her arms wide and let her wingspan fingers read the braille below the corresponding letters on the doors, marking the rooms. She learned the alphabet with her eyes closed. She was assumed blind by her more reclusive neighbors and kept stranger to them.

By the following Sunday, Sara had translated three more letters. They became her semi-daily rewards, a new hobby. She found herself stopping to read and then reread every public piece of braille she could get her fingers on.

This slowed her day down enough, just enough to get through it. She memorized by sight every letter in the Braille alphabet, she memorized it using her accounting skills. The ability to associate a pattern with a number, and then that number with a letter. It was slow going at first, like a child with a new language. She did enjoy that aspect, taking deep breaths and being patient with herself. She became nostalgic for her first word spoken (what was it) and the first step she took as a child (did she fall soon after) for learning this new innocence. She read her found Braille with her eyes open, silently mouthing odd storefront business hours and hotel elevator instructions. Soon after with her eyes closed she let her fingers find and attempt to decipher the bumps. She whispered the letters to hear the language.

Come Sunday Sara decided to share two of her favorite translated letters with Colleen at their weekly dinner. She felt as if the letters had propped open a door only artists get to travel through, a door that she could not yet traverse, but only peer into. At first, it was difficult to decide which two letters to bring.

"I found something ... or some things ... some letters. They aren't dated, and I don't really know who they belong to." Sara told Colleen after they placed their orders at their usual table that night. "They're written in braille and I want to read one to you, and, trust me, I want you to close your eyes when I do."

"Oh yeah?" replied Colleen, lightly smiling, like a wine glass rolling on its side.

"Yeah, kind of think of it like a game," Sara said.

Sara then read the first of her two favorite found letters from Henry. She read it eyes closed with her favorite fingers at the slowed racing pace of her learning curve. Whether or not Colleen opened her eyes to peak mid letter was lost to Sara. Sara only really wanted to share it this way, in a sightless conversation, as most all letters sent are originally shared. Colleen did peak at Sara in the beginning. She could not tell whether Sara was truly reading the braille blind or rereading the letter from memory, perhaps a bit of both. It was somewhere in the second paragraph that Colleen gave up on figuring out such a truth. In fact, just before Sara's fingers ran dry of the bumpy sentenced road they traveled upon, Colleen found the corners of her lips breaking wide in a sightless happiness, a blind smile.

The letter read, read as follows:

Dear Lillith,

We have come to burning all of the money here. That was all it took in the end. It smells like any other kind of paper, but it feels like so much more. They came for our money so we burned it. They came back and they filled our fireplace with candle sticks. It is a beautiful irony. And the wax smells wonderful. If there is ever a place in this world for the efficiency of failure, it is within our chimneys. It is the fact that great things are capable of failure that seems to scare them. We are great things.

I want you to know when I walk I write your name in the hardened cement with my white cane. I write it over and over again, and the I's and L's in Lillith clear my path. I swing and tie the letters together in a cursive handwriting. *Your I's and L's, they keep me safe. These things may come to leave you, these letters, they bounce when you write cheques, for me, they are my EKG, my heart monitor. If only a piece of chalk graced the tip of my cane, the world of this city would know of you. That is the difference, a piece of chalk at the tip of a blind man's cane. That is, I have decided, what missing wants, a piece of chalk to write it, what is missing. Are you batting your eyelashes? It is surely harder to find them worse than better surprised. Does this letter let them flicker? I would catch butterflies in my hands to feel better. To find and know them sooner than you, to feel them. I will be leaving here soon, and I can say I will be coming to you. After burning all of my money I have found a pricelessness in that statement, and it is in truth.*

    Your love, Henry

After waking from Henry's letter's dream, Sara and Colleen came to find their waiter waiting over them, their hot meals in tow, his tall straight frame and the pure energy of his impatience apparently failing to penetrate the arresting nature of Henry's writing. He did not mean to stop them or speak up, did not hope to utter any bit of a cough while Sara read. He assumed they were caught in some new type of religious prayer. This patience of his did, however, catch the attention of the four guests at the two tables on either side of Sara and Colleen. It was most likely the sight and smell of the two steaming hot dishes that got those two tables to stop talking. It was then Sara's voice and the letter she read that got them to listen.

Sara's voice was beautiful now lost, and as it kissed the unknown pitfalls of her language's new stumbling typeface, they found it (coupled with the letter) most arresting. The letter wasn't after all loud or brazen or violent. It was the reading of it, and its strange homilies that left her voice in a different radio frequency than the other banal chatter. It held an outstanding weight of life. While Sara read, the four guests at the two adjacent tables glanced at the girls. They did so peripherally, to avoid the awkward feeling one experiences when looking upon someone who cannot meet you with sight in response.

"Can you please keep it down?" One of the tables thought to say, and yet retracted upon finding Sara's voice was likely the softest and lightest in the cafe. "I thought it was interesting," a woman at the other table wanted to reply. Though such a comment would invoke an admittance of guilt to spying, and the woman feared it out of bounds.

After apologizing to their waiter and accepting their dinners, Colleen finally responded to the letter read, the letter she heard. "Wow Sara, that's really something. This Henry, he really sounds like something. That must be fiction, what a writer, that couldn't be real, burning money blindly? Chalk on the end of a blind man's cane?"

"I don't think it is fiction though," Sara replied, "I think the truth is trying too hard for it to be fiction," she stopped and collected breath. "It doesn't have to be. I think he really could have been, just, endlessly hopeful ... just off in this place trying to support his love from far away, off in this terrible place."

The accidental eavesdroppers at the surrounding tables failed miserably to pick up their own conversations. They had no idea where they had left off. As soon as these conversations began again they did so feeling halfhearted, like those of secret service agents faking all too commonplace topics.

"So you think it's all real, then?" Colleen asked.

"I think because he is blind it very well can be. Let me show you. That was only one letter, but I brought another one, let me read it to you." Sara loved this, she had Colleen more than enthused. Colleen the artist at the end of her seat, Sara the accountant presenting the art, and though it was not her own art, she felt it was, in a buried treasure sort of sense.

"Read it blind again," Colleen urged while Sara pulled out the second letter. Colleen held her wine glass to her lips and, eyes closed, took a very soft and silent sip.

Sara did read it blind. She read it from the celebrated work of her bitten tongue, and Colleen listened, and the two tables around them listened as well.

My Lillith,

I have taken to dragging potted plants under all of my roof leaks. I heard them dripping onto the floor of my loft after the first storm. I found their puddles with my bare feet. I have found five leaks and I have only five plants. I certainly hope this does not get worse. It does my apartment well to live with these plants. It does me well. I love the smell of their growth and the matted sound of a roof leaking into loose loamy packed earth it is a precious soft one. I do suppose if another leak should come to fall I will fill a cooking pot with soil and wait for an unknown growth, gracious for a lost seed. I sometimes live in a greenhouse of suspicions, a small garden of opportunities. I dream they are growing only to someday plug the holes that feed them.

Let me tell you, it is easy to run a bath when your house may be flooding from the sky down. It gave me some sense of authority. I wanted the water here, now, enough, stop. After the bathtub was full and the rain kept on coming down I got in, slowly. I took a straw to breathe with me. With my whole body under I pretended to be just another houseplant. You would say I was giving up my responsibilities. I suppose I was. I was so still I couldn't hear anything. My legs and arms became roots. Can you see them? I couldn't smell anything but I knew the storm was here. I could feel it. I knew it was everywhere, without being able to know anything. I think the houseplants felt the same way. It wasn't a bad feeling. I wish I could share it with you. If you get a chance, you should get into a tub of water when it's raining outside and only breathe through a straw. Can you imagine it? I do miss you and I hope your weather is not so ragged as mine is, I hope you can feel the sun on your face.

Your love, Henry.

In the communal bathtub on the third floor of the Alphabet Hotel, Sara pinched her bottom lip into a fold thinking. She cleared her loose eyebrows through an aimless tugging with wonder. The plastic straw she stole from the cafe lingered between her two longest fingers and rolled up and down them like a cigarette, or a pen. She had translated all of the letters but one. She wrote out copies and gave them to Colleen. Colleen wanted to do a series of paintings or sculptures, mixed mediums, one for each letter. Sara held her tongue at dinner when she thought to call such an activity fan art. She held her tongue knowing that she planned on going back to the hotel and submerging herself into the bathtub and trying to be a house plant in a storm, to meditate, if nothing else.

She thought of Henry often now, knowing he was never one of the various blind men she saw walking down Market Street. She wanted them to be him. Their heads down, their white canes EKGs. She wondered what they were writing, were they writing anything? She knew Henry thought of her as often as they did, which was never, because just like Henry they could not see her. There was a silence to that distance. It felt very much like being lost.

She rushed home some days to read the letters, which seemed to break the silence, and that to her was a beautiful sound. She gave up on the island of her mattress. She spent her nights sleeping on a raft of collected soft things. She did not consider it drowning, more learning how to swim. She no longer wore her silver rings, the weight of them too much for the required sensitivity of the found public braille she so enjoyed reading. She became the girl that has to touch everything, that strangers assume ripe in fingers fluent in flu and germs.

Some nights she found nightmares, in which Henry's last letter simply read, "I want to see you," over and over again. She thought about that all day after that first night. "I want to see you," written in Braille, over and over again.

She did read the last letter, one week later. She read it blind on accident assuming it to be one of the others, lost at the top of the pile in plain sight and unmarked. It read late night easy, like a prayer to leaving, her eyes closed and hands pressing play. She still swears it isn't fiction.

Dear Lillith,

What if we were all mostly broken? They've moved us into large dorms. I cannot sleep here. Could you? I woke up in the middle of the night to nine other men all snoring in different notes and rhythms. They all have big old broken seashells for noses, all crashing into one another. It could have been a symphony in another world. Can you hear that one? We have been sleeping on waterbeds, and are blessed regularly with our buoyancy. We are each regaled to our own some semblance of captainship. And upon these water beds with the snoring sound of the ocean I drift in close enough to be just far away from you.

We never found out what was in those old factories we cleaned out. We have been told we are finally finished. We are trading hopes as to what we have accomplished. Then, we speak of who left, and who is leaving. I learned a new word today, mirage, it is something in the distance that you can see that is not truly there. Most often it is something beautiful. I was also told everything looks better from a distance. You do look quite good from here. I am fortunate to only really know you as these letters do, from an arm's length. Perhaps I will never know a mirage, though I am accepting your exceptions when I sleep. I hope you sleep well.

Your love, Henry

The Cherry in Spite of You

"I found blood in the sink again," Maria told Scott.

And those words reminded him of three weeks prior when he had bit into the first cherry of his life, in a jazz bar off Sixteenth Street, after holding out for thirty years.

The bathroom they shared while getting ready for bed was a small seven-by-four, all tile and echoes. They once made love with her sitting up on that sink, in the first week. It destroyed his grin every time he brushed his teeth from then on. The hymns she made that night bounced off the walls and back into him, into his ears, into his mouth, even into his teeth.

"Oh, yeah, I bit my lip at work." He responded. "There was this woman on the phone that was going on endlessly with 'umm' and 'uhhh,' it was the worst. I just started chewing on my lip, and by the time I had taken down all of her information and her increasingly long credit card stuff, I just had nothing left. I'm sorry. The stress shouldn't have gotten to me. I guess when I was brushing my teeth it broke back open."

"Were you brushing your lips, too?" she asked him with impatient sarcasm, the kind usually reserved for the latter end of a relationship.

. . . .

He wasn't lying to her or to himself yet. Three weeks earlier in that Jazz club, he found himself staring at the shoulder blades of a beautiful woman. The shoulder blades, the neck line, and the back of her neck, which, for all good reason in such a cold climate, should have been covered instead of coveted.

It was freezing outside, and she was backless in Alaska.

That night, in that jazz club though, after finishing his third Manhattan-a drink he had resigned himself to after ten years of whiskey-cokes-he found himself chewing deeply and hideously at his cheek. After five minutes of chewing and staring, chewing on his cheek, and staring at her neck, the last song by the last jazz setup had finished. As this woman (later to be Maria) began to clap along with the rest of the crowd, Scott took in his last view of such a back line for quite possibly ever.

Scott studied psychology, loosely. His mind was the last thing he sought to figure out in his twenties when he still sought to figure things out. He knew association. He knew loss and he knew tight knots, and holding hands the way that synapses do. He had, however, never, by a combination of chance and texture, ingested a single cherry.

Scott, fully aware of the sweet and amorous reputation of cherries in general, quickly placed the sad whiskey-soaked cherry from the bottom of his Manhattan into his mouth. His hungry teeth let off his bitten cheek as well as his bitten lip, and as he stared into her back line he took one deep chew into the cherry and let the pulp remain. Then, he bit again. He had tasted cherry flavored drinks and cakes before, but never the pure fruit. Now though, he had to let it reside in his left cheek, until she walked away, when he could swallow it down. For as long as she existed the first time, the cherry must exist, and as soon as she was gone, the cherry must be as well.

He then spent his walk home to his single apartment spitting up various textures of red, mostly, though not distinctly, bits of cherry and blood.

. . . .

"You're always grinding your teeth," Maria said next.

. . . .

And these words reminded Scott of the first day they finally met in a café, finally met, though it was the very next day. She was one patron ahead of him and eager. She was still backless, strapless, her jacket caught upon a hook fastened tightly to her hips.

"Can you hear that?" she asked the customer between her and Scott.

"Hear what?" the customer asked.

"It sounds like grinding, or frustration or impatience."

"Sounds like Monday morning," the other customer said.

It was the sound of Scott's teeth destroying cherries, reaffirming the association of her. He found them in a parfait the café was selling and self-serving, assuming the customers weren't up for stealing.

Scott, overhearing all of this, stopped. He stopped because he was grinding his teeth, because the cherries were mashed and bleeding. He stopped because the association was alive and breathing.

"Never mind," she said, "I think it stopped."

Scott made his usual purchase, a double shot of espresso, plus the parfait, and he didn't even have to speak of it, which worked out quite well considering all the cherries that he had been hiding. The double shot of espresso was his first association, one he had made for his current employer. The strong distaste and sharp bitterness had fueled him through the classified ads.

His luck led him, laptop open, to the seat behind her, where they sat back to back. Today was his day off, and days off were spent looking to find a new job; that someday might lead to more days off. However, in attempting to produce more days off by finding a new job, he found the few that he had disqualified themselves.

"Excuse me," she said to him, with her upper body back line curved, "do you smell cherries?"

. . . .

"I can't sleep," Maria finally announced.

. . . .

This reminded him of the first time she made this announcement. Though this would be, at last, the last statement she would speak while they were together.

The first time she said, "I can't sleep," he mumbled, "go to bed," but he said it so softly.

It reminded him because he said everything softly in his sleep, because he had to wear a mouth guard, because she had reminded him endlessly of cherries, much like the first and last two that he would ever eat.

See, Scott had hoped this girl, Maria, would have disappeared after that night in the jazz club. Then whenever he wanted to come to find her back line, all he would have to do is sit at home and grind out a couple of cherries.

The association was simple: the pulp, her beauty, and his teeth.

Yet, at the café that day, the day after the first cherry, the day of two cherries, they started talking. Then, after three weeks of dating, all he could think of was her neck as they slept spooning, and all he could do was grind his teeth, in thought of cherries.

What else could he do, as he lay there, her bare neck directly in view, the last thing he saw before closing his eyes to sleep?

At the end of three weeks, however, it felt like all she ever said was, "I can't sleep," and, "you're always grinding your teeth."

So he left, and he swore off cherries, and he swore off Maria. He stopped drinking Manhattans, and instead of hitting up his favorite jazz club off Sixteenth, he headed to a strip club in North Beach.

. . . .

"You're not you anymore," Maria said to him, which were words he could never remember hearing.

That night at the strip club, after talking with one of the ladies, and then waiting after her shift was over to possibly get a drink with her, the bouncer punched Scott square in the jaw. He went down quickly. Then he limped home to Sixteenth, which was strange because his legs were fine, only his mouth was bleeding. Where his mouth was bleeding, his lips were torn. His bottom jaw was pushed a quarter of an inch to the left, but he didn't lose any teeth. Upon his arrival home Scott found upon his doorstep a beautiful woman with a very large jacket covering most all of her back, yet her name was still Maria.

"You're not you anymore," Maria said.

Which were words he could never remember hearing.

However, the quarter inch the bouncers' fist had pushed his jaw off track has ever since kept Scott's teeth from grinding. Now, when Scott orders his Manhattans, he asks the bartender to kindly hold the cherry, in spite of Maria.

Depluralize the Pair

"This is too hard."

It came from the kitchen, before the door shut, with only one foot up over our threshold. She said it before she even saw me. She was waiting by the sink with her left hand on her hip while the right one held her up, anchoring her on the edge of our two square feet of counter space. What was it though? Had she given up? Colleen, that's an interesting kind of pain. There was hair under her fingernails, the small white down that blankets the bottom of her earlobes.

"James, this is too hard."

A couple hours earlier I was on the corner of a grocer and a bus stop, a place of heavy foot traffic. At first I thought it was all a joke, but then I learned about "the process," the signatures, the wrist flicks. There was a group of what seemed to be college-aged students collecting signatures to ban what was referred to as "The Mislabeling of Coconut Juice." Half the people passing by didn't bother listening to or reading what was being pushed.

They simply signed, just dragging their hands across, as if shooing away the invite, the bother.

"Campaign against coconut milk!" the group yelled.

These people simply spotted the Red Cross canvassers and took opposite ends of the street. Then they crossed whenever the Red Cross workers would, as if in mirror juxtaposition, always remaining at lateral ends. I hated them for this.

"This was white on white crime, this was just plain stupid." I told my wife while unloading the groceries, ignoring her previous comment.

"So what you're telling me is that there are these people who organize and volunteer their time to ban the idea of coconut milk? They want it frowned upon? That from now on it's coconut juice or ignorance milk?"

"Yes, and they are doing it with steadfast political premise. They have flags and hate slogans."

"Hate slogans?" she asked.

We moved around the countertop island in the middle of the kitchen as if sparring, staying at our own lateral ends. To throw a punch was to pull something from the grocery bag.

"'You can't milk a nut', and, 'juice is to fruit, milk is to us!'" Just repeating these lines made me feel used, like a commercial actor paid in the product alone, or like a prostitute paid in sex.

"I don't think that's a hate slogan. Did they have a mob? Was there an angry coconut mob?"

"There were three or four of them on that corner, enough to be obnoxious. It's just, I was watching the Red Cross workers and they looked ashamed. I mean, they were trying to save lives. Anyway, here's what I did, and why I was two hours late to dinner, and why I think we shouldn't get a divorce."

With this she pulled up one of the two barstools and perched at the end of the countertop island, sat up straight and went all listen to the witness on me.

. . . .

We met in the 1970, at a rally for the take home pregnancy test. The rally was for modern art. When it first came out, giddy like children with new toys to piss on, to lay claim to, to legally bind with DNA, my friend Mike and I went out and bought one. For the sake of sarcasm we placed two items upon the counter of the pharmacy that day-one box of spermicidal condoms, and one three pack of home pregnancy tests. Staring up at the clerk, so proud of our irony, we both reached for our wallets and waited for the total. We watched with eyes wide, wondering if the clerk got the joke, wondering if he understood the ball was now in his court, his pharmacy was now our prank shop.

When we got back to the dorm I had an idea to take the whole thing a step further. I unwrapped a condom and slid it over an unused pregnancy test.

The lubrication aiding the testing point down the ribbed for her pleasure stairs, where it seemed to find every step.

"Get it?" I asked Mike. "Get it?"

"You are definitely on to something," he stopped for a second. "I like this. It's like the baby is trapped in this technology. This cold sterile rubber and plastic thing, farthest from nature and romance and skin and warmth and piss and cum and life. I like this. What do we do with it?"

I thought about it, about relationships. They always progress or end in ceremonies. Divorce or marriage. You always need a witness or two. Since the condom and the pregnancy test had only just met, we needed to marry them as soon as possible. We needed witnesses.

"Okay, I have an idea. Get on the phone. We need to schedule an impromptu field trip to the Museum of Modern Art. I need numbers, at least twenty or thirty kids outside the Museum in half an hour."

I went about sawing a window into the front cover of the pregnancy test box, then covered it with a clear plastic screen. It looked like a child's matchbox driveway for a new tiny race car, except inside I parked the pregnancy test wearing the condom. It was a small diorama, or the future of marketing, it was an ad campaign, it was as loud as a billboard, and I held it in my hand.

At two in the afternoon Mike called me back and told me the rally was set for three. We were in luck, it was Memorial Day and MoMA was already quite busy with visitors. I thought at first to bring signs, to march the new piece into the gallery like a prisoner of war, handcuffed inside of itself. I decided, instead, to go with a briefcase to keep it rich, classy, anonymous.

I arrived at two forty-five with the brief case and Mike waved me down. He set up a sort of podium. Really, he only turned over an old crate in front of the crowd for me to stand on.

"Here's the plan: You unveil it, walk in with it, place it where you think it belongs in the museum, then walk out without it. I've instructed our crowd pretty much one by one of this plan. We're near fifty strong so I'm sure you won't be given any trouble."

Littering is littering because the item or items left behind are devoid of value. If you leave a dollar bill on the ground it is not litter, it is luck. We employed this idea on its head, a condom and a pregnancy test, separately useless, yet combined worth a discussion at least, thus not worthless.

I gazed over the crowd of art students. I wasn't entirely positive they knew what they were getting into. It's easier to be a part of something than to be something.

The crate was not the least bit sturdy, and it was hot enough to make my socks feel wet inside out. Had I washed them? I stepped up. I didn't even say anything, I just held the case above my head and opened it like a toothless jaw mouth, bright red velvet on the inside, the box in the throat. I felt like I was selling futuristic toothpaste, maybe even an answer. I wasn't. I was selling a joke, a criticism, Art.

The crowd cheered and Mike put his long arms in the air and waved everyone in. After years at the Art Institute we got to know the door guy and dropped him a stack of twenties, tens, fives, and some ones.

I vanished into the middle of the crowd. We moved piece by piece, with the briefcase safe at my side. Having seen it all before we had to put on the guise that we hadn't. We played amnesia for the security cameras. I traveled in step with a young female student I thought quite pretty. I peeked at her to my left; she was tall and thin with brownish red slightly curling but mostly just wild hair. It seemed as if she dressed in a manner of merely throwing clothing. It was an experiment, wearing what stayed, what stuck, her Velcro fashion. The clothes she kept. Her purse was a large loose bag of autumn colored fabric, most likely home made, the straps were long and thick, almost just rope. Her fingernails were painted haphazardly, every other and speckled. They looked hit by a fire hose on the wrong day, like it made a good story, and there was her proof.

She stopped me at the urinal, not the museums restroom, but that one famous urinal. It was French, it was Marcel Duchamp, and it was his Fountain. Back in the nineteen forties Marcel was told any of his pieces to an upcoming featured art show would be accepted. He decided to drop off a urinal. He called it "found art" and then raised a fit when they refused to show it. I thought it was ridiculous, though hilarious. Years later it was lost and commissioned to be recreated eight times and shown throughout the world at various modern art museums.

"I never really understood this," I said to her. "The piece is so crass, it's the statement that was art."

Staring down at my briefcase, I knew I was no different, but I wanted to be a part of something without being it. My piece would be anonymous. She bent over to tie her shoe and I watched as her hands bypassed her feet altogether. She had a long skirt made of rust green, brown, and blue four-inch squares quilted together. On one knee, she worked something metal out of her purse-a shiny flat box about ten inches around with a dial in the center. It was a bathroom scale.

"Smallest one on the market," she told me, "I needed it to fit." She then placed it inside the urinal, or should I say Fountain by Mr. Duchamp.

I stepped back, and it was beautiful. She was measuring waste, she was making a statement about the statement. I thought about the utterly rich, the accountants, the anorexics, and the weight trainers all measuring their excrement. I thought about the cliché of calling someone anal. It was just waiting for her here, too, the base of her piece. All she needed to do was drop the scale in. She stood up and stepped back as well, cracking her knuckles on her jaw. "I like it, I saw this last week and thought it could use something. There, now, much better. Why is it so busy here today anyway, is there a new opening?"

"Oh," I glanced up at her, her Irish eyes green, her eyes' green iris, her iris green. "Yeah, I mean no, there's a good amount here for something else."

I then bent over to tie my shoe and while on one knee removed the box from my briefcase. Before I stood up I glanced at her. She was beautiful lost staring off at some pastels on the wall.

I put the condom fitted pregnancy test on the bathroom scale in the urinal in the West hall of the Modern Art museum. I wanted to call it the sequel, or the future. We had married not only the condom and the pregnancy test but the scale and the urinal as well. It was a shotgun wedding, no doubt. When I stepped back it felt like everything, like the human condition.

I knew what it was though, the child, the waste, the weight, and the shame.

I closed my brief case and held out my hand, "My name is James, yours?"

I didn't think to mention what I had done to her modification, I wanted her to see it, but without her knowing I was the guilty party.

"Colleen." She then glanced down at my additions. "Hmm." She pulled the test stick out of its box and laid it condom and all so it made a V with the box on the scale.

"There, I think it's done now."

She wiped the slick oil lubrication left on her hand to the side of her skirt, where stains go to dye.

On the scale, the test stick looked sad, a dead bagged seal drying up on a beach. Hope seemed lost for it, its plastic casing once promised a use in medical supplies, then demoted to this, it looked the lowest.

"Now it's so sad." I told her, "But true."

"James, if this is all we ever make I'm okay with that, just don't tell me this was hard. We should probably get out of here before someone notices."

"Agreed, want to catch a drink somewhere?"

"Sure."

. . . .

The last to be unloaded from the grocery bags were two bottles of Asti, her favorite champagne, which she fawned over neck bent sideways, telling me to get on with it. Her chopping board was already all ready on the island, her knife in tow, ring finger sandwiches a late night addition to the menu. I popped the cork on the first bottle and took a deep drink, knowing the carbonation would buy me time. Hiccups in a court room, your Honor. I handed her the bottle and began my examination.

"This is how you break your legs waiting," I began, "I stood on the wrong side of the street for half an hour after pledging ten dollars a month for the next two years to the Red Cross canvassers merely out of sympathy. The Coconut Juicers didn't even have vests, like the Red Cross guys did. So I went into the craft store and bought them vests, all white, like cowboy doctors, 'White like coconut juice, right,' I told them, 'unity, now you guys are united.'

They seemed mildly confused by the gesture.

So I went and bought them fresh coconuts too, and a corkscrew.

'Look man, if you want to help you can grab a clipboard and start collecting signatures,' one of them said to me.

I considered it; I would simply swap the signatures for a campaign to depluralize the pear, the lonely pear.

'You can finally buy one pear! A singular pear! Peer is one! Pear is two!' I would yell it from across the street, with their coconut clipboards grasped firmly between my fingers and palm.

I decided that would be fun, though ultimately fruitless."

"Or fruitful?" she buts in, her head cocked, asking me if I get the joke.

I nod in truth and continue, "Besides was I really ready for the radicals that would sign up to single out the pear?"

The lonely pear.

She shook her head and drank more, not yet laughing, not yet not.

"Instead I stayed back working the corkscrew into the coconuts." With this I showed her my palms red, and worn. I mapped the calluses like focal points to my story with my index finger.

"James…" she started up, "don't you think we're getting kind of old for this?" Her pajamas had faded throughout the years. Her night dress was now relieved of all creative duties. She wore plain white drawstring sweat pants and my old work shirts. She once painted her white slips in red wines with fingertip brushes, their thin rivers running down her legs.

I will admit through age that I became afraid of the insides of her knees. The way she no longer took two steps at one time going up stairs, something I always loved about her was now gone.

"That's just it, let me finish and I'll tell you why we aren't too old for this, and why we shouldn't get divorced."

The cheese in our fridge was molding right now, right over this conversation.

· · · ·

She worked on the IUCN Red list; these are the people that decided what species are endangered, threatened, and extinct. She quit the day the Ocelot was moved to "not threatened," as if escaping a burning building with her cats.

I told her I would marry her for money the day she walked out on that job.

I told her we can open a magic shop and when the rent goes missing unapologetically exclaim it had indeed disappeared, with wands in our hands the landlord would have no choice but to believe us.

She told me that makes about as much sense as going to bed with a mattress salesman.

I was designing the plastic rabbits that dogs would chase at the horse race tracks. I was streamlining want, and I was pushing desire. I spent a month testing different sizes, small enough to fit in their mouths, large enough to see speeding off into the distance. We married in a cave on a day we ran out of words, playing a game we called Lazarus.

"Constituent"

"Seethe"

"Unmuzzeled"

"Indicative"

"Reach"

"Dissertation"

These were our favorite words; and we shouted them down into an echoing well deep in a cave off the coast of California. We shouted them down and they would come howling back upon us in and out of this tomb, back to life, just like Lazarus.

"Is this harder?" I asked her, "I don't see this getting hard."

"No." She always capitalized the N when she said "No."

Our Modern Art installment had made the papers. The pictures taken of our "subsequent graffiti" had become the art, then the newspaper it was featured in became the art. It transversed mediums, mutating like a virus with no host, a child with no parent or home. We did keep it close to us. The sixth page of the local section of the Examiner where it featured was framed and hung on the back of our front door. We were late to work some days, caught reading it again and again.

"This is easy," she said on her toes, "don't you ever tell me this is hard."

"All right then." I began to follow her out of the cave and became caught up watching the strands of hair that eluded her ponytail and tickled the back of her neck. They swayed and pecked like detection whiskers.

"Wait," she said suddenly, stopped by the vague and appalling sense of an untied shoe. She wore sandals with thin aged brown leather binding. She bent down on one knee. Earlier that day she had tied an old bronze ring to the strap separating her biggest toe from the rest, it kicked and bounced back and forth that afternoon. Now untied and freed she pressed it around not my ring but my pinky finger, the only place we found it fit.

"I just wanted to get that out of the way before we left the cave, you know, like Lazarus, alive again upon departure."

Enter to exit.

I was later told she grew her nails out for that single day, her first married dinner, like so many women before her, all cuticles.

. . . .

We were getting older, we were. She would understand this better if she heard it a hundred times, and yet she has never. Why would she? Her forever-crumpled single dollar bills, caught like Kleenex at the bottom of her purse, she was still young, she had to be.

I shaved my head at the first sight of a gray hair, and that was ten years ago. She had asked me if I considered dying. I asked her if she had ever thought about death. She said, your hair, considered dying your hair.

We were getting older, we were.

She asked me about my thoughts on cremation, I reminded her I was lactose intolerant.

"I worked the corkscrew into five coconuts then began to pour them into cups of shaved ice. This is the weird part though, all but one of the coconut canvassers abstained from the fresh juice. They were mostly repulsed by it. The one guy that did drink it was just a ninny, he had no backbone, didn't even enjoy it, gagged a little even."

"No..." She let out a sigh of sarcasm.

"It gets better," I retort.

I hid my dirty clothes at the bottom of one of the grocery bags, I had a clean pair left from the end of the work week to change into on the way over in the car. Their white stains were violent enough to belong at the bottom, to belong hidden.

You can never start a conversation with violent white stains, or it becomes much more, it becomes an explanation.

Was this harder though? All of our conversations became explanations. Where have you been? Your hands are caught red. I was five years older than she was. She mentioned the lack of windows in our apartment, she said we could use a skylight or two, something to look forward to, to look out of.

. . . .

We decided to wait till we both had the hiccups to record the greeting on our answering machine. "Leave, your, message, after, the, hiccup, now, no, now. No…" then laughter and more hiccups.

. . . .

At the time she was working for a nonprofit called "Hairsy." They collected hair as donations for a nunnery, or a collection of nunneries, or just the Catholic Church. She herself was agnostic. The hair was to be made into wigs for the nuns who were fighting various forms cancer and chemo. Women were more likely to give their hair to sisters, she told me.

I was painting that blue stripe you see on Greyhound busses as they drove by.

We lived these lives as if merely trying on different hats at a thrift store, posing in front of mirrors.

We wanted everything to be art in some way or another, and innocent, though most of all youthful. We put Band-Aids on each other's freckles and referred to them as time scars. It was denial. It was denial in the same way you brush your teeth real hard before you go to the dentist, as if the damage, the neglect, is reversible. It was a penance. It was finally all coming to a head. I didn't think my coconut story would save us. We finally had to deal with something hard, that wasn't artsy or youthful or innocent.

"I went ahead and, well…" I reached inside the grocery bag and pulled out the stained pants and shirt. Stained like murder stained, story stained, explanation stained, excitement stained. "…coconuts are compostable. I gave away the remainder of the juice and shaved ice drinks to the three or four homeless people who were asking for spare change in front of the grocer. Coconuts are compostable. I went back for the shells, the husks, the meat, the milk, the juice, and flesh. I tried a number of conventional methods. First prying them open with the corkscrew jammed into the holes I made to drain them, but I had no leverage. The corkscrew tip merely kicking around like a child's legs underwater. Next I attempted to weaken the shell with a small grid of holes drilled, which proved long winded and ultimately fruitless."

"Fruitful!" She perks up again, not yet bored, amused by herself.

"Same joke, same hour?" I ask.

"Different fruit." She tells me.

"I found a rock though, a big one, with a blunt end and a sharp end, it sort of resembled an oversized arrowhead. I brought the rock over to the drained coconuts and began to drive them into it one by one. With every crash I felt this round hard shell give in my hands a little more," I made my hands into a large cup, as if holding a ball. "They split first into hairline fractures, then shattering cracks. As they broke through, and occasionally got away from me, I strangely felt stronger than I should have. The meat and milk of it spraying me as I went along. It felt murderously good, and I was so lost in it, so lost in it that I didn't notice both the coconut canvassers and the rest of the crowd at the intersection were watching me. They gawked at me like I was having some kind of breakdown. And I was…"

"Were you James? Because I wish I were invited."

"i was," I told her, and when I told her I used only lowercase letters.

If you lived here though, you'd never be home. We lived farther from the truth.

"The truth was that the mislabeling of coconut milk and juice had taken a couple of peoples' lives due to allergic reactions. And I had no idea. The difference was in the age, the juice being fresh, and youthful. The milk diluted cream pressed out from the thick, white flesh of a well-matured coconut, the difference was in the age." I told her again. "and I had no idea, and there's this thing about the unknown, but I haven't figured it out yet. They told me about the allergic reactions after my breakdown, They assumed I lost someone to the juice. That this was merely a case of post coconut stress disorder."

I started to capitalize my letters of intent, and I think she felt them.

"This was why the canvassers shied away from the fresh drinks I had prepared, my best defense now defenseless. I thought of them as silly hipsters. That they were attempting a grandiose investigation on a banal fruit's texture, its consistency, their rights to challenge nonsense. Like we once did in a modern art museum downtown. College does things to people. Soon after they packed up their posts I signed their petition, and I'm sure it will make the ballot in November. It wasn't easy I'll tell you that, but it was true."

I thought about freshly planted trees that needed wooden planks to stand up. I thought about paper coupons that advertise paper sales. All this mark up, all this useless.

About three hundred million cells die in your body every minute, of natural causes, of life.

I took my dirty clothes to the laundry room, down the hall just before our one bedroom. I placed first the detergent then the stained shirt and pants. I set the washer's dial to lights even though the clothes were dark, the white stains now accounting for the majority of the clothes surface area. Colleen followed expressionless, jaw ready, though knife down.

"I can't…" She started, then stopped, a barrage of adorable champagne supplied burps disabling her protest.

"I know." I told her.

I bent over to check the dryer for warm clean clothes. My knees creaked. I knew I couldn't paint busses forever. We were without witnesses, this ceremony could not go on.

We were older.

We did have champagne.

We once protested the Ms. Alaska Pageant. Well, we only really scoffed at the swimsuit competition from our couch while it played on some public access channel that we clearly should not have had access to. I mean who swims in Alaska? We just wanted a good old sled dog competition instead. We wanted to see their hands make that awkward cupped robotic wave while they rode by in heavy as hiding jackets. We wanted these fragile women to yell "Mush!" or whatever it is they yell at dogs in Alaska to make them run faster. We wanted to see them grit their teeth. Their strongest smiles in the utmost upturned corners of their Vaseline mouths.

This is who we were.

I smiled and took her hand. I found her youngest thumb on her right hand. I circled her fingernail stopping farthest from the outer ridge, this being where she was the most young now. I kissed it and headed back out to the kitchen to make her dinner, finger sandwiches with or without rings.

Weak Nights

I

Apartment 30

"I certainly wish my heart would slow down," she sang to her parrot nine times that night in her one bedroom apartment. Her voice was lighter than she meant it to be, and her parrot was better at mimicking her tone than her words. She placed a thick crocheted blanket over his cage in an effort to dampen her voice, to make it deeper. The blanket only ever made him fall asleep though, which she found out ten minutes into her private speech repetition classes, her songbird classes, she called them. She would slowly lift the blanket, drawing the curtain of light back up, up to the roof of the cage, only to find her new parrot sleeping standing up. She decided they were just power naps. Then when he did wake up he always came to say, still soft as ever, "I certainly wish my heart would slow down."

It was a powerful thing for a bird to say in such a small space.

It was all the parrot knew.

She cradled her voice throughout the room, never singing always sung. Her colleague at the zoo joked weeks ago, "You should pick up a talking bird, you should pick up a couple of talking birds, you could teach them to sing. If anyone has the voice to turn talking birds into singing birds, I'd say it was you."

She was lonely at best, worst case kept busy blowing the steam off the head of her coffee. It wasn't much to ask of her, to adopt some birds, to keep some company. It was important to her to have someone else in the room when she said things like, "It's a good thing I exist."

To be honest she felt as if she owed it to the animal kingdom after being hired at the local zoo a couple of months earlier. She was hired as the "Main Feeder," which was a title. The kind of title that keeps one from updating their resume, like Emperor. She got the job interview through her sister's husband's father. The far reaching hand of an in-law leaving her far reaching hands in the jaws of a lion. As the main feeder she mostly fed the lions and tigers, mostly fed them raw meat. She was good at it though, with her arms always as outstretched as true happiness.

She was a complete stranger to the phrase, "You're throwing them to the lions."

She adopted one parrot, a male, to start, and snuck him one midnight up three floors to her apartment, apartment number 30. The parrot had a blue coat with a bright yellow breast, his beak curved sharp. She placed a white sheet over his broad round brassy metallic cage. She took the stairs in fear of him imitating the elevators' hum after they exited her floor. She listened to every step in the stairwell. At first she felt that sneaking a talking bird into a permanent place with a prerequisite for being quiet seemed foolish. That is until she spotted some movers hauling an upright piano into the apartment next door.

Her new parrot would have taken better to her singing if she sang, which she found out she couldn't, all too late. What she said next to her parrot was the same thing she said to those lions with four pounds of sirloin in her thick rubber gloved hands.

She said, "Bird, your eyes are so bright, I certainly wish my heart would slow down," except to her it sounded like a song.

It was the same thing she said to herself in the mirror the morning before her interview.

"Bird, your eyes are so bright, I certainly wish my heart would slow down."

It was all she could think of as she signed page after page of legal documents releasing the zoo of all liability should she be hurt, maimed or killed as their Main Feeder.

"Bird, your eyes are so bright, I certainly wish my heart would slow down."

It wasn't a song until it got her out the door every morning and it wasn't an anthem until it gave her the courage to sign her life away. It became a prayer everyday she met the lions and tigers who roared so loud no one else could hear her.

On the fifth night a pair of policemen knocked on her door due to a disturbance call that was meant for down the hall. "Bird, your eyes are so bright, I certainly wish my heart would slow down," was all they heard, though not from her. It was from the soft felt of a now well-trained bird, and they responded the only way they knew how.

"Is everything all right in here?"

"I'm not quite sure, to be honest." She told them with a faint smile in a soft voice like a song. Her hands were folded in her lap, and her head was slightly bowed.

II

Apartment 32

They sat around a small circular table in the kitchen of their two bedroom apartment, a newly married couple, with the window open, smoking a cigarette each. They had just put their first child of sixteen months to bed.

"I can't call, it's too early, it's only nine thirty at night, and you have to admit it sounds kind of nice. Maybe it'll be good for her, maybe she'll grow up to be a prodigy because of this."

"All I'm saying is if our baby wakes up and starts screaming again, it's your turn to call."

"This will be the fourth night we've called, we don't even know who this new neighbor is."

A new neighbor moved in while they were away on their first vacation since having the baby. They finally decided the baby was old enough to be left at the husband's mother's house for a week while they were away. They went to a cabin on the coast, listened to the waves and drank red wine.

Upon their third night back, it began at roughly eight o'clock and ended fifteen minutes after they called the police. It was a piano playing next door.

"Okay, I'm calling them at ten. It's a week night."

The husband crossed his fingers that both the baby would not wake by ten, and that the piano would stop at ten.

On the day of their child's birth they promised each other, for both the baby's health and their own, that at the end of each work day they would split one bottle of wine and have one cigarette each, only one.

She knew he was relaxed when he stopped re-corking the bottle after each pour, which usually occurred three quarters through. He stopped re-corking the bottle three quarters in figuring, at that point, the wine was more so enjoyed than the possibility of its remains being spoiled.

He laid his head back against the screen of the window and closed his eyes, turning his head to spill the smoke.

She watched the baby monitor that only ever made sounds.

Apartment 34

After the armed robbery of a small jazz cafe on Sixteenth Street and the subsequent four gun shots that were fired several feet from his head, he lost all hearing. The police report notes he was found under the same baby grand he had played in that cafe for the past twelve years.

After the incident his sister moved him into a cheaper apartment down the street from her, not knowing how much assistance he would need after spending his entire life listening.

While moving his piano into this new apartment, she was asked if she would have it retuned. She replied that she would, though ultimately failed to see a point, and didn't.

He told her he needed some time alone and that the settlement from the criminal case was enough for him to live off for a couple of years.

The first couple days he couldn't think to play music.

He went out and bought six white canvases and a set of paints.

He relished his sight after going deaf.

He hated his first four paintings. The other two canvases stayed white.

He couldn't sleep. In a fit of terrible silence one night, he painted the entire spectrum of light across all fifty-two white piano keys. Every octave blending in an out of its seven steps of brilliance. The arrangement as a whole composed a rainbow, and as far as he could tell the strokes of his paintbrush were too light to produce a sound. It felt good though.

This feels good, he said.

The next night, after the paint dried, he played the colors, he played them like he was painting, until the police came.

"I am sorry I am deaf," he wrote on a scrap of paper for them, not willing to speak, not caring for noise.

They wrote back, "You can't be playing this late."

He wrote, "Okay I am sorry."

He didn't have a clock, and after all of the insomnia he didn't want one.

The police left soon after, pointing to their watches with their heads down.

Apartment 32

"Maybe we should move out of the city," she said.

"We met here," he said.

They always wanted to be the parents strong enough to stay, the ones that didn't go back to the suburbs, like their own parents.

Their cigarettes were half burnt through, and only being allowed one they each used their own tactics to make them last. After sixteen months they never thought to share these tactics with each other.

At nine fifty the baby hiccuped in her sleep, and the wife heard it through the monitor. The husband did not. He went on listening to the piano from the apartment next door.

"Maybe we can switch rooms. We'll take the nursery and we can move the little one into the master, away from the noisy neighbor," the husband said.

"That means he wins," she said.

He stared at his cigarette for the time.

She stared at the clock, her cigarette almost out.

Apartment 34

He stopped opening his eyes when he played the colors on the keys, but he still saw them, as he played them, from the back of his head.

They splashed loud, then faded out like the music he had known his entire life.

He left the door unlocked and cracked open knowing he would not be able to hear the police knocking. The police knew not to knock now, and they didn't mind telling an old deaf man it was time to go to bed. They even began to stand in the hallway for a couple of minutes listening to him play before walking in and tapping him on the shoulder, then pointing again at their watches.

At this he would turn on his piano bench, press his hands together, and with a slight bow thank them for their kindness and understanding. A gesture he was no stranger to, after years of an audible applause.

III

Apartment 36

They finished by nearly eight o'clock every weeknight in May. They promised they put their pens down, they said their goodnights, and they hung up their phones.

They met in art school, in a sketching class fifteen years ago. One day the teacher asked the students to think of the one student in the room they recognized the least, and to close their eyes, and to sketch them. They only had ten minutes. She set a timer, and after ten minutes she ordered their pens down.

Once finished the students were told to write the coordinates for the seat of the drawn student in a battleship or bingo fashion on the back of the sketch.

The drawings were then placed in an anonymous pile for the drawn subjects to sort through and retrieve.

"This is what you look like to someone in this room that knows you the least." The teacher went on to say. "Does this look like you? Can you tell who drew it?" she asked. Some of the students didn't receive sketches at all, their faces too common, they had, "One of those faces." Some of them received three or four sketches. They had to take this lightly, winning the least recognizable lottery.

This couple that lived in Apartment 36, they drew each other that day, perfectly. They went on to refer to each other as their seat coordinates, he was D3, and she was F7. D3 waited outside the classroom that day, astounded by the likeness of himself with his drawing. D3 had tiresome black caterpillar eyebrows that climbed his brow, he had a widows peak she found just as enterprising. F7 had jet black dyed hair the perfect length, she claimed, to sweep chips of angst and unhappiness from her shoulders. When F7 met eyes with the boy she drew she couldn't help but lift her lip the littlest bit. D3 then spotted his drawing in her hand. It was all over.

They became chronic artists, they became lovers, they became facial composite composers also known as crime suspect sketch artists. They moved in together and worked together at the police station. They competed. They drew the police chief laughing at their love. The lesser white stains on his shirts were always exaggerated.

In May F7 was transferred for a month upstate. She was chosen over D3 as the artist to work a high profile serial killer case. The high profile serial killer had the most generous face, he gave it to a record number of witnesses. While she was away F7 feared she may sketch this terrible man more than anyone else in her entire life. She called D3 in apartment 36 every weeknight at seven o'clock. She called him, and she asked him how his day was, and what he had for lunch. He told her about a new neighbor that plays the piano, and some bird feathers he found in the stairwell. He asked her what she was wearing and how many times she had to tie her troublesome left shoe that day. She drew him doing their laundry. He drew her returning her rental car. They bought each other these empty books before she left. Every night they added one more drawing of each other, if only to stay recognizable, to be the one they knew the most. The books became built like day calendars, of lovers doing mundane things.

At the end of the month with the serial killer still at large, F7 complained to her supervisor that she could not see to draw this suspect anymore, that she may not be the best artist for the job. Her wrist began to shake when his description came to view in her minds' eye, her blue eyes almost watering. The department called up the second best available forensic artist in the state to take her place, which was her husband, D3. He took the train up, afraid of flying. She flew down, tired of upstates constant driving.

F7 arrived home, tired and lonely to an empty apartment 36 after a month of being away, her yawns tasting distinctly like airplane air and the inside of her lungs. She was sad to see their twin drafting tables trade dust from these uneven bouts of use. She soon felt better when she found upon their bed two black sketchbooks, one empty labeled June, and one full of her, signed "D3" and labeled May.

Where Pickled Jalapeños Grow

for Grandpa Bill Taylor

She misplaced her trauma through running, pressing the seconds into the ground, her long legs time-stamped away hours.

"My shoes are coming off!" she yelled as the front door finished its crescendo; first the brass section hinges all worn down to different notes, then the beaten air of a slammed door drum.

The tile was colder than she expected. She wished nothing more than to agitate her household with bare feet and slammed doors. Though she did place her black dress slip-ons safely to the side to keep from obstructing anything.

The funeral was two hours earlier and the overbearing heat of a church parking lot led her astray. She remembered that she forgot the ice tea in the fridge at her home two miles away, and excuses were just that to her, she was free. Besides, the air-conditioned car and the acceleration of escape in her right foot felt like running, and she had not run in twenty years. She did roll the window down, and she did close her eyes anywhere past thirty-five miles per hour or third gear, whichever came first.

Of course, she knew the route home, she knew the traffic, she knew the speed and everything came effortlessly, everything except for breathing and blinking. That is what the pressing stream of air was for, flushed upon her face, and why she needed to close her eyes.

The funeral was her husband's. He passed one week earlier while sleeping next to her. The events of that night led her to stay at their lake house the following week, only returning home to attend the funeral.

It wasn't his death that led her away to the lake; it was the sleep walking.

It wasn't his death that scared her either, it was the way her husband carried himself so unconsciously to his old oak desk catty corner from their bed. He was a Halloween ghost that took off his white sheets. Once there, hovering over the tucked-in chair, he mumbled what he attempted to write out, which she could not begin to understand. He then carried himself back into their bed and under the covers, now a Halloween ghost within his sheets, back to sleep before he passed sometime that night.

She spent all week wondering when he stopped living. Was it directly after the trip to the desk, or hours later?

She spent all week wondering what he mumbled and meant to write.

She spent night after night waking from dreams of his lifeless hand, naked of a pen, dancing to the beat of misplaced syllables and mutterings. Her mind time-stamped him standing there in a sagging off-white undershirt and old, vertically striped, blue and white pajama pants.

She had seen a sailor lost at sea.

She spent all week trying to remember if he had ever walked or talked in his sleep during their fifty-five year marriage.

If he ever did sleepwalk, she certainly must have been asleep while he did. She was a very deep sleeper. He had called her a rock in a hard place the mornings she slept in and would not leave their bed for even a fire or a flood.

"Flood?" she had said, "this is Arizona; say drought."

"Why would you leave your house in a drought? It is much more dry outside," he had returned.

Now, barefoot, she slowly walked down the entranceway to the kitchen to the left. Every step left a warm, wet breath of her life on the tiles, sometimes bridging the grout with her feet, crossing borders initially left forever separated (though mostly staying within the lines). She hasn't opened her fridge since his death. Her friend Debbie tended to her house while she was away.

At first glance she thought to leave the pickled jalapeños. They were his favorite; he would draw them from the jar then down his throat like a sword-swallower, head tilted back, neck straight.

Throughout the entirety of their relationship the sight of pickled jalapeños gave her headaches. She spent a lifetime asking him, "Who eats jalapeños in this desert heat?" It disgusted her.

"These are going, now!" She yelled as her clammy hands choked the jar and tossed it, not into the wastebasket, but straight out the window above the sink and into the garden. The glass shattered and in two hours the neighborhood cats will lick it, then their paws, then the glass again.

She could have fallen fast or slow, she could never remember it the way she hoped. The action was lost in the weight of falling, the weight of vertigo, the result, the floor. She fell from the springs in her diving board ankles, for running and jumping was once easy. She had come from a long line of women with strong thighs and long legs; she was his baby giraffe.

In two years in a rest home she would brag about the coldest part of her house. She spoke at lengths about how it changed her life, just how she landed in it, five feet out from her refrigerator. She landed deep in the center of her linoleum ocean. She was lost at sea, in the center of gravity of her home, the belly button of it. To say she could not wade and dig into the surface would not keep her from pressing further into the tile. She did so until it was no longer cold. Then she swam two feet to the left and traded that cold for her warmth. She wanted to drown though, to put all the willing parts of her body to sleep. She was done trading warmth, wanted to get all the Arizona heat out of her.

After several hours of swimming through the cold linoleum the doorbell rang and she jumped to gather herself. It was Debbie, her friend, her house sitter.

"Jean, are you okay? Is everything all right? Did you still want to do John Wayne Sundays?"

She felt like a fake, like a recovering alcoholic drinking everything out of his wine glasses, brandy snifters, and champagne flutes.

He brought her flowers before every date for the first year they were together, even though she was then a florist.

She stole five vases before she just started planting the flowers in the garden where, fifty years later, the pickled jalapeños would grow.

He would tease her; "You're taking your work home with you."

She would water them five times a day, the only flower bed in Arizona.

He would tell her, "That's us," when he found something beautiful in the middle of nowhere.

John Wayne Sundays were a weekly ritual her husband, Debbie and Debbie's husband Paul would take part in. Every Sunday they would gather around the TV turn it over to AMC and watch The Duke do his thing. She could not watch The Duke today; she decided then that she could not watch The Duke ever again. In truth he had always secretly reminded her of her husband. Her husband's name was Bill or William but never Billy.

"Jean, The Duke misses you," Debbie yelled through the thick front door while peering through the abstract stained glass window.

She will not respond to these demands, not today. She hovered squat with her knees just inches from her teeth. Her back to the wall, east of where the hallway ends, just out of view, like a bank robber. She was, however, without his favorite expression, his six-shooter, his Smith & Wesson.

She eyed the junk drawer across the kitchen, across the linoleum ocean she only just drowned in, and waded towards it. Once there, she began to search for something. She was crouched beneath an excuse, a reason, a justification for a gun in a shoot out. She searched with only her hands, and her hands searched with only her fingers. She found a staple gun, some thumb tacks, and a pad of paper that soaked up the blood from her fingers prodding at the thumbtacks.

"Jean, I know you're in there. Look everyone just wants to know you're okay … Jean will you just let us come in?" Debbie shouted.

Debbie said, "us." Debbie was not alone.

"Hey Billy, can you hear me?" Jean yelled back, still crouched, tracing a map of the house on the tile with her finger. She's cased this bank of memories for the past half century, she dreamed of hitting the vault they made in the bedroom. She drew out the escape routes, she motioned down hallways to guest bedrooms.

She's seen this movie, she knows this hostage negotiation.

Jean stood her ground, staple gun in hand.

Secretly grinning inside her clenched teeth she perspired from only the nerves on her forehead.

She checks her gun twice, loaded as always, he must have left it for just this occasion. She was his cowgirl.

She grew up twice.

First in Arizona, second in his eyes.

She grew in elation, on her toes to see over roses and into his eyes.

He wore a wide-brimmed hat, and had just returned from fishing. He tilted his hat in her presence, just like The Duke does, though he had never seen any of John Wayne's movies. She wore tacky, yellow gardening gloves and a beat up canvas apron. She spent the day trimming roses and removing thorns.

"How much for some of those thorns?"

"I'm sorry, we don't sell the thorns." She stood with her hands in her lap, head down, hair up and held loose in a bonnet.

"Can I buy some roses with thorns?"

"I see. I suppose I can just give you the thorns, but why, what for?"

"That's all right. I'll take one dozen roses with thorns."

He gave up fishing with metal hooks and lures, finding the idea to be cruel and uncreative. He liked to work with his hands, threading the fishing line through the thorns over and over again. It looked medieval when he was finished, and with pride, he took full credit for every catch.

She sold him the roses and threw in a free bag of thorns with little to no negotiation. He liked that so much that he came back the next day and asked if any other flowers had thorns.

She told him that nothing had been easier than pulling those thorns out. He assured her nothing had been more difficult than putting them back into the fish.

This day, however, everything was difficult. She started with her little toe that began to pretend to get her out of bed. He had named her smallest toes his tugboats. It all led up to her last panic breath, right before she fell asleep in the cold white linoleum waves of her kitchen floor, not but a couple of hours ago.

Now Debbie, and now demands, and now she is so adamantly displaced. She is thinking of the words oratory and gesticulate, and the game of Bridge she lost to him the night he passed. She is thinking of what it means to win anything, why they count stairs in flights, and all the energy he wasted living in a two story home. He might have aged differently had he not been so fond of flying her up those stairs in his arms every night after their wedding day for the great length of their marriage. Now she was his flightless bird, anchored to the bottom floor.

The staple gun in her hand became wet and clammy. She thought about fingerprints in all those heist movies, they must be so easy to dust, all those assailants just sweating out the evidence. They're crying guilt. She wondered how long it will be until Debbie would leave, or if more relatives would show up. She pictured paddy wagon headlights staring into her living room, a small barricade, someone in a suit with a bullhorn. She imagined the neighbors pouring out of their homes, someone setting up a lemonade stand to combat the heat. It was a Sunday so cotton terry robes must be prevalent, and slippers too. Questions come out with the neighbors, they're all center stage for a shootout. She is her own hostage, and she is her own bank robber.

"Hey Billy, can you hear me?" Her voice this time cracked and her yell came at a much weaker volume. He's never responded to Billy, and this is why she called it, to free the silence of guilt and quiet.

Then more knocking at the door, and the glass sounds thicker and safer than she previously supposed. She thought of the bruises left on the knuckles of its tormenters, then she smiled a little.

Of course she understands the demands of her objectors outside, her staple gun, however, most certainly does not, and she wears this well, this fear that she's been provided with, her hands shaking just enough.

"What would The Duke do? Where is my Sundance Kid? He always said I shot more like Butch. He was always my Sundance Kid."

"Jean, please ..." Debbie now sounding desperate. Will she call off the rescue party and go home, or come back with an army?

Is it still a rescue party if it fails?

She thought about the longest bank robbery in history. At what point do they refer to it as a war? Then she thought about the longest hostage negotiation. Do the hostages remain friends after the event? Do they wish to never see each other again?

Were there wind chimes in hurricanes?

In Stockholm, could there be any other syndromes?

"I'm staying," she then yelled with an awkward pause, the words not knowing they knew each other, new to one another, like another new language.

She thought again about his last words, his late night ghost mumbles. Do they count if he said them in his dreams, or are his last words "Goodnight," which he said every night for the last fifty-five years, whether she was a rock in a hard place or not?

Perhaps they count more, his sleeping words. They are surely composed of a random sampling of his synapses firing with no outside influence. They are entirely grown in his own garden, himself endlessly.

She slept well that night and remembers dreaming of him. He was in his huge fishing boots, and she was in just her stockings. They were young again. They were in the desert. The sand burned her small feet so she stepped up upon her toes, then up onto the toes of his boots, There she held him with both her hands on his hips, she was his anchor, and he her ship. They then began to walk out away from the scorching hot sand, but it felt more like dancing to travel so close to someone else, to travel in one's hands. Then, before she knew it, they were dancing, and it was the fastest way to go home, her weight on his biggest toes, his tugboats.

All of this comes back, and now all of her, all alone. Though her face was red, she was not blushing. She does not blush. This is Arizona, and she will tell you that she sunburns quite easily. To her feet, to her feet and with her staple gun.

She approached the hall strong, and opened the door coolly, her staple gun in hand, her long legs in tow. She became the greatest escape from herself, and from her home.

Outside a hot breeze dusted her car with a layer of sand that outlined the oily ridges her thumbprints left on the door handles, which was proof of her driving there. The hot sun caked the rubber from her tires deep into the black asphalt, leaving her car's fingerprints here as well. Her blood was left on a pad of paper in the kitchen drawer. Her DNA is splayed about this crime scene where she robbed herself of her old life.

She dropped the staple gun on the porch, and slowly raised her arms. She kept them visible at all times to a non-existent crowd of her own imaginary country western demands. Leaving the staple gun on the ground, she got into her car and drove away. After fifty years of putting everything in its place. She was off into the desert, into the sunset.

The credits never rolled, but a missing persons report was filed. When the police did search her home this evidence was, alone, enough. She existed enough, and there was nothing he could have said that last night he hadn't already said to her, enough.

"The first few hours," she told me, "of a heist, a robbery, a murder, a funeral or a wedding, are always the worst. Everyone is on edge as if we forgot our lines, lost our stage lights. We just want to fall back into the earth and get the warmth out. To surrender to vertigo. To cool down. Just breathe slowly and retreat. I breathe the same whether running or sleeping, for most of my life I couldn't tell the difference. Doctors say my lungs are stronger, and my nerves are shot. I really can't tell you what happened that day. I can tell you what I think, and well, what the evidence shows. Then there's what the police told me. They said it was enough to book me on some kind of robbery." She will smile when she gets out that last line.

. . . .

In Arizona there's a rest home owned by Pat Stacy, John Wayne's former secretary, whom he was allegedly romantically involved with, which she presupposes in her biography titled "Duke: A Love Story." The rest home is called "The Alamo," and all the women who once loved a cowboy go there to fall asleep, and all the men who believed themselves to be cowboys go there to hang their hats. The Alamo looks spot-on like any Western movie set in Hollywood, or like Arizona in the late eighteen-hundreds.

These long lost widows and widowers all claim they'll never forget The Alamo. It's where all of the television screens play black-and-white westerns. You can hear the housemates tell their stories of when they rescued themselves. Ask Jean hers, and she will tell you about walking out to an empty street with a staple gun in her hand. She will tell you about John Wayne Sundays, and Halloweens dressed as Cowboys. She won't cry or embellish. She will beat you at Bridge, but she only sleeps on the bottom floor of the home. She's not afraid of the stairs, she may have simply forgotten how to climb them. Now retired this feels enough like home, to be grounded in this fantasy, and to swear against the god awful heat. She is, however, she says, forever, surrounded by witnesses, and a jar of pickled jalapeños.

Ten Fingers Ten Toes

A couple of years of ago I asked mom why she doesn't make tea anymore. She told me she was, "emotionally unavailable." What an adult thing to say, I remember thinking, "emotionally unavailable." She should have at least said it while pointing a finger, or with her tongue out.

At the time I thought this was nothing that a big jar of pickles wouldn't fix. In the long run, with our short legs, this was supposed to be just another mishap. We would race into the kitchen. Our hands were still small enough to claw out the best of the jar. We were a combination of eights, nines, tens and one eleven. At such a young age I remember birthdays the same way we counted on our fingers, we were consistently staring at the ones we had to leave behind. When we were eight we didn't know what to do with our pinkies, both of them. When we were nine we felt incomplete. We were almost entirely covering both of our hands. We had one left. It wasn't overwhelming, we knew about our toes, bending over twice a week in gym class, being told to touch them. I knew about them. Someday I would count on them too. They were our insurance.

Sara, Beth and David were knocking at my door. They didn't ride their bikes which means we were most likely going out to the train tracks. I wasn't entirely sure who made these decisions, as I was always the last one to be picked up. My house was on the way to either the park, the dried up canal, or the train tracks. My mother told me I should have a "laundry list" of things done if I wanted to go out, but she does all the laundry in the house. I knew I had to clean my room which mostly means moving things around. I had to finish my homework. "Everything is homework," I would tell her, "do you see me doing it anywhere else?" I couldn't tell, but I think she was glad I pronounced our house to be a home. "It's almost raining outside," she told me, "what are you kids going to do out in the rain? Catch colds?"

I took my vitamins and doubled up on orange juice that morning with such religion, I thought it may slip by her. She does so many things with such religion, or ritual, or routine. My mom, she doesn't worry so much as she proceeds endlessly with religious amounts of caution. Like, say, after dad left she would only buy me thick knee high socks, which worked out great for my rain boots, but I always had to fold them over and over my feet when I wore shorts and tennis shoes. They called them tennis shoes but I'd never played tennis in them, in fact I'd never played tennis at all. So I showed her the length of my socks, then untucked and re-tucked my boots into my pants, and my gloves into my sleeves. I left no skin showing, save my face. Everything was airtight. I remember secretly enjoying that feeling. I knew in my short life that this was as close as I would come to being dressed as an astronaut. I remember pulling my hood over just before she leaned in to kiss my forehead. The drawstrings in both of my hands, pretending they were the cords pulled on a parachute, leaving me leaving her.

"I'm so glad you keep your pocket in your pants," she had said to me.

"I'll be back early if I get wet, we're just going to the park." I yelled while I ran out.

I knew the storm was coming, it would be the first of the season. I found out last night, it was on the five o'clock news. For my birthday that year I asked for a can of Scotch Guard and stayed up every night before any storm prediction, spraying down the clothes I would wear the next day. My hands have never been more steady as they worked the can up and down my jeans, my sleeves, and my hood. I wanted to believe that spray had made me bulletproof, I wanted to believe I was in a lair, and I was a superhero. I have no idea why they call it Scotch Guard though. It protects against moisture, and how moisture can protect against moisture also befuddled me. I remember Grandpa always saying befuddled a lot. I stole that from him. As far as I know scotch is only something adults drink too. I supposed scotch being a liquid Scotch Guard would protect against it, but I missed something somewhere. Anyway, thanks to Scotch Guard, telling her I'd be back as soon as I got wet quickly became one of my favorite truths.

I knew It simply would not happen. Besides maybe she could have used a little more trust in me. She didn't know that every time I threw my socks into the laundry, I made it. I made it on the first try, from across the room.

David flagged me with his arms to hurry up, which was easy for him, he's the oldest, he turned eleven that week and finally reached for his toes. He was also by far the tallest. I suppose we're all lucky in our own right. Sara was the youngest at eight, I was nine, and Beth ten. There were odd combinations of authority bestowed among the four of us, best ideas won debates outright, regardless of age or height. After that, the deciding factor was height, then age.

Age came into play when I wore my tennis shoes or Beth wore her sandals. We were deadlocked in the spring because I had cut what my mom was calling my winter hair. The tuft on the upper back of my scalp proved beneficial against her long golden flat hair that ran down easy to her shoulders. We would measure our heights back to back with an unbiased judge directly after any and all disagreements or decisions on who gets to pick first in certain games. Somedays, I would grow taller throughout the day, losing decisions in the morning to win them at night. We put so much weight into our height, it was such an easy need to grow up.

"Come on," David yelled up the driveway.

They all took off running as soon as they saw me. I would have to catch them. Before I knew it, we were sprinting down the street, racing up and down the curb, in and out of the gutter. In running I threw my feet farther and farther from my body, almost leaping, so as to stretch them, to make me taller. We ran down the block and through the strip mall parking lot behind the department stores to the loading docks where the eighteen-wheelers took their shipments. Once there, and out of breath, we made our conversations staring at the concrete floor, bent over with our hands cupping the balls of our skinny knees, glancing up from time to time at our next challenge: the wall. We only ever just called it "The Wall." The wall was eight feet of cinderblock. Behind the wall were the train tracks where we would play combinations of tag, freeze tag, hide and go seek and long jump. Long jump wasn't so much a game as it is a ritual, a jumping off point for the day. Of course David held the record, he was the tallest, second place was long mine.

Climbing the wall was the easy part, we had a system. The finger and footholds we used were sparse enough to be celebrated upon discovery, yet ultimately regaled proudly with routine. The getting down though, that was the hard part for me. We had to jump down, and for this there was no routine. I had tried various methods of a coordinated fall, because that's all this was, my best shot at doing something that could someday kill me. I say this because grandma fell last year and it killed her. She didn't even fall from the top of a wall, she just fell in her kitchen and broke bones and bled on the inside. I mean I know she was really old and mom says she did so much in her life. Grandpa seems okay. He seems okay, he's always saying things like "I thought you would," and, "I figured as much." His declarations have become so soft, he became such a big softie. It's not like I was afraid of heights because of this, just afraid of falling.

That day though, the dry summer had piled up thick sharp yellow brushy tumbleweeds, resting-no-longer-tumble, right where I usually made my most calculated fall.

"I am, I think," I said, "getting better at this," mostly, consistently, only, under my breath though.

David jumped down about five feet over from my spot on the wall. He is an acrobat if you ask me. And I'll tell you because where he jumped down it's probably even farther down than eight feet. He tells me the dirt is softer over there. When he lands he just goes into this fantastic tumble roll. He told me he would teach it to me when I turned ten, that I'll use my whole body to do this roll, even my toes.

When he told me this it felt like I had no idea what my toes were for, I had no idea what I was walking on.

Both Sara and Beth did this lazy dangle thing that usually results in them scraping either their knees, (when they wore skirts) or their jeans (where their knees should be). They slowly lowered themselves, fingers gripping the top, until there is roughly four feet from them and the ground. Then they would scream real quick when they fell. They only screamed for as long as right after they let go up until right when their feet hit the ground. I wonder if grandma screamed when she fell, I wonder if guys ever scream when they fall.

I was usually the last one down from the wall, and that day was no different. I remember thinking mostly about mom's smile when she said, "Be careful." I always thought of important things when I was on top of the wall, or when I was on the diving board at the club house pool in the middle of the neighborhood where David lives. I remember wondering if when I did get taller I would only ever think about important things, like I would always be on some kind of a wall, or some kind of a diving board. Anyway, I was thinking about mom's smile and the thing about it was she never went three dimples when she smiled anymore. After saying, be careful, she totally only went one and a half, maybe two dimples when she smiled, the obvious easy dimples, the ones she didn't have to work for.

I could see pretty far from up there. I couldn't see my house, but I could see the street leading up to it, the one we ran down. I could see all the clouds coming in for the first terrible storm of the season. If you asked me it was no coincidence that school started the same time the weather got all ugly like that.

"Hurry up and jump!" David yelled up at me while dusting off his jeans. Both Sarah and Beth were picking golden thistles from their jeans, almost in the same casual manner they would someday paint their nails as women, making small talk with their heads down, hands busy, like mom did on the phone. I usually did some kind of countdown, sometimes ten-seconds, sometimes just a three-two-one. That day though, since my usual landing was covered in tumbleweeds and now evocative of a major life decision in my brief nine years of living, I found myself pacing back and forth.

This was the worst thing I knew to do. To wait. It's when you stop lying and just wait. Mom waited through winter that year and plucked all the petals from the roses she had grown, she steeped them in hot apple cider whenever the temperature dipped below forty degrees, or whenever she or I had a sniffle. She did it as a substitute for tea, because Dad had managed a tea shop, "Into the ground," last summer. Which I thought was a good thing, because tea grew from the ground? Those were grandpa's words, "Into the ground," and that's why I use them, but I think I was missing something here, too.

I walked once again to the end of the wall. David, Beth and Sara were all about twenty feet down the tracks practicing their long jumps at a ten foot stretch we had cleared earlier this summer for mostly only that purpose. Trains stopped running through there about two years ago so the brush grew dense and perfect for hide and go seek. Since I was dressed covered head to toe, gloves and all, I pretty much conquered any threat of splinters and thistles. I was, I remember, at that point, basically superior in every way, except for the falling. To simply jump into those tumbleweeds, though, reminded me of something dad would say. He'd say if you fell into luck enough gravity wouldn't be such a misfortune. I found myself fidgeting with my sweatshirt zipper. I wanted to know how many teeth were in it. I wanted to stop in the same place every time like the combination of my locker at school.

"He's not jumping today," David yelled, "he's gone and got himself caught. Somebody better call the fire department. He's stuck."

The next thing, I guess I forgot to remember. I walked over to the part of the wall where David usually jumps and just let myself go. I attempted to mimic everything I saw him do that summer. I wanted that roll he did. I wanted to use my toes to grow up. I pictured my muscles as rolling mechanisms. They were gears, timed and firing perfectly. However, in my attempt to forgo not yet being ten, and my not knowing what exactly my toes were for, or what I was doing, or how to use anything properly, I let go and broke both of my thumbs.

. . . .

The next thing I do remember is waking up next to my mom in the hospital, without pain. The first thing I felt were my mom's fingernails on my forearm, and that can hurt. She leaned over me at my elbows, entirely blocking the view of my hands, which felt sealed in cement blocks. I remember thinking I wasn't going to make it to the first day of school. I couldn't write with these block hands, I couldn't even hold a book. I'm starting the season on the disabled list for sure.

Sara, Beth and David were in the waiting room reading each other their horoscopes from yesterdays left over newspaper. Horoscopes in a hospital waiting room, of all the places to find them. I like to think they would have read mine if they remembered my birthday. I wonder if it would have alluded to anything.

My mom, she was blushing past lions when I opened my eyes. I hadn't seen her that red since Christmas. She did lose a couple tears, but she also went all three dimples, a sight I had missed myself. I thought for a second, maybe it's better when you make mistakes. This fall brought us together, like grandma's fall did. Grandpa was there too, he leaned up against a wall in a red sweater with his arms folded. Dad would have said something like he had apparently practiced and purchased the all important posture of apathy at the hospital cafeteria. Wait, where was dad?

The doctor said the breaks were nearly impossible considering their perfect symmetry and simplicity. He said that the casts shouldn't be on longer than two months. We believed every word, they were all so new to us in this context. He said I did the impossible.

He gave me a thumbs up after he said that, after I broke both my thumbs.

After the doctor left my mom finally moved aside so I could see my hands. They were both stuck in the thumbs up position wrapped white and rigid. The doctor may have been mocking me. He said they would be thumbs up for the next two months. What resolve, I thought. I felt a slight champion, a thumb war veteran or something. She told me that after I fell I went into shock. Then David called 911 at the Party City. I was so jealous. I always wanted to call 911, and calling it at Party City, what a mess. She asked me if I felt any pain. I said no. She said good. I asked her where dad was, she said on his way. I said good. I guess these thumbs will have to stay broken, there is no difficulty in this truth. I hadn't seen dad in months, I couldn't wait.

The scars still run up and intertwine with wrinkles and fold lines. They are symmetrical, and I show them off as long as they will last. I show them off when girls ask to read my palms, and I end up telling them this story. My favorite part was when I asked my mom what the doctor meant when he said I went into shock. She said it meant I ran out of pain. Which kind of sounds like being "emotionally unavailable." She said it's important that some things always hurt. I usually tell girls it's important that this always hurts. When I tell them that I push my opposing fingers into where the scars are. Then I fake wince a little bit when I do. Which is kind of like lying, but my dad says it's more like dipping tomatoes in ketchup at this point.

Together Selfishly

She must own tile floors. The sound of a woman's lithe barefoot walk in the morning from her bed to the kitchen is not unlike the quiet steady presence of a house cat. It is one to behold. It is pliant. Her sleepwear will follow her nonchalantly to brew coffee or tea. Once there and waiting she will gaze at one of three things: a window's view, a mirror, or an old photograph of her mother.

She will come to question, while gazing, the order of her current top three priorities: her health, her future, and what is to be done with the naked body of a young man nearly half her age lying-possibly faking sleep-in her bed. Her two longest fingers walk and leap from one freckle to the next on her opposite forearm, marking them.

The young man will lie in her bed listening. He is not asleep. He will shut out all his senses except for his hearing. He will listen for her next move. He will listen for three things: doors opening or closing, clothes finding or leaving her body, as well as the caution or aggression of these actions. He will hear three things while listening: he will hear her experience, her trust, and her interest. If she is good, he will hear nothing but the altruistic necessity of her bare feet finding and then leaving the tile floor, her bones perfectly quiet. Whole centuries for the two of them exist within this quiet. This quiet makes the tea kettle a train whistle, it is the Chinese water torture of the coffee pot brewing. If it were raining outside they may have been married in a couple of years. If there was thunder they'd have died in each other's arms. In a tornado she would not have left the bed to begin with. Instead, on this Sunday they will have this silence, together. She is one of those women that listens with her mouth just slightly open, ready to purge her thought. He listens best holding his breath, in order to quiet his lungs.

Her name is Hannah. She is currently unkempt at best, wearing her Sunday worst (him) all over this (her) bed. His name is Jeff. He is wearing his best (her) as she stalks the hallways looking for a noise, though not her own, to get him out of her bed.

This silence though, they spend several lifetimes listening to it rest. What once would have kept them together they are now dying to let loudly live.

This is theirs, their first possession, whole heartedly shared.

He fears an itch that climbs the lower half of his left calf, perhaps a spider or a leg cramp. Her eyes water and dart when her tongue is burnt by her morning tea, it is loose leaf chamomile for her hangover, pushed silently through a french press.

Last night he met her by way of brushing her lost eyelashes with his right thumb from the top of her left cheek. He asked her what time it was at 10:10, then 11:11, then 12:12, in a weak attempt of falsifying a stutter she never had. She had taken multiple trips to the bathroom to free her smallest toes from her fishnet tights, she regarded them as her smallest fish. He, in turn, regarded these trips as an insecurity, as she did return endlessly with her hair slightly more perfect. He did, however, in the taxi to her apartment, repeal these ideals weighing his gradual and inevitable increase in intoxication.

She stopped applying her usual mascara earlier that week as a friend had informed her of its ill effects upon an animal in a part of the world she would never visit yet wanted to in some way. This boycott was simply the best she could do to save it, to save her chances of someday visiting it. Now without the weight of her ill-reputed mascara, her eyes fluttered lightly, shaking off loose lashes, as if useless feathers.

In the morning in the kitchen she stands upon her left leg, her right heel pressed to the inside of her left knee, fitting it perfectly. Her elbows are bent to hold a single mug of tea at forty-five degrees. She is burgeoning angles all the while he (eyes buried) fakes sleep. She plays (blow) press the steam to the window, and with this discovery heat she replaces the misplaced fingerprints that other people from previous house parties came to leave.

She opens the kitchen window. He rolls over. She slams it as if to disagree. He nudges her pillow. She gathers up a towel and takes a shower.

While she is in the shower he rolls in and out of her deciduous sheets, leaving him, leaving her, leaving this, with a fight, without spite. He is up upon the first sound of the shower door closing, and quickly speeds up his dressing upon hearing it close the second time knowing she is now merely toweling off. He searches her smallest drawer for one dark clean sock, to match the one he lost.

The night before, upon returning to her apartment, they drank three quarters of a bottle of month-old Rosé wine, both likening it to pink lemonade.

Their drunk tongues spilled the wine like children throughout their mouths, laughing eyes wet at the oncoming summer of morning while dancing down the moon in their respective Saturday nights best.

He studied anthropology, leaving his thumbprints in the concave accepting joints of various human donor skeletons. His evidence always left after the fact. He studied bone structure and the chemicals that comprised them. He preferred where the upper leg met the hip, and the tight taut fit of the elbow.

She pressed through college bound to several ballet scholarships, studying psychology, wondering why it felt so good to point her biggest toe straight up to the sky. While they were in bed something happened. Sometime last night and before this morning after years of stretching and pressing her bones, all of her joints came round to perfect circles. This was together their best unknown, though he did presuppose it. And it didn't need to happen to anyone, but it did. Her every bone orbiting its adjacent, mirroring life to a T, every bit of calcium slow dancing to perfection inside of her. It was an eclipse of chemicals he would spend the rest of his life trying to describe in bars and operating rooms to strangers, coworkers, classmates and colleagues. Sometimes he would speak of her triumphantly, sometimes depressingly harsh. This was her winning lottery. Her grace to leave the world, though to her entirely unknown, and only really lasting one night.

A certain kind of cinderella, and it's easy to miss one's perfection, never knowing it had hit.

She left the bathroom towel pressed and wet, having freed herself of his finger and lip printed kissing. She was destroying proper evidence. The careful almost archeological love he left on her found precious things now scrubbed clean. She is reticent and leaning this morning, everything is forward or back in this moment. She may speak of their past (last night) or their future (his leaving) only.

In the kitchen upon hearing the tell of the bathroom knob he glanced over to find her wrapped and dry. He is dressed merely in pants and boots. His shirt is lost between her headboard and mattress, a matching white with her sheets. He is caught nearly finishing the last quarter of last night's Rosé.

He is celebrating (her) his find.

"You know," he started up, "when they judge these wines they talk about it's age and where it's from and it's grapes and terroir, but the ones tasting it, they never mention those people. I think it's incredibly one-sided."

"Look..." she took a short breath.

"The thing is," he cut her off, "these judges, these tasters, they're old in seniority to the wine game, their tongues are life drunk, they're aged sour, they wouldn't know perfection."

"Are you still drunk?" she asked.

He is hesitant to mention her perfect bones, his find, his dig, their second something paired with the silence they owned-which is now dying. He thinks she is Cinderella in a shoe factory. Her all-new-all-something, is nothing without his credibility. It is null and void. He will instead relate her to wine, right under her nose, as he drinks the wine right under his.

"Every wine peaks..." he started again.

She cannot tell him all the things he did right last night to land himself here. She would be validating his parking in her bed. If she did he may think himself welcome back, and that she could not have.

"I am not," he smirked, "drunk. What time is it?" he asked.

He asked this as a sort of trick question, the analog clock above her bed sat perched permanently at twelve. She was not tall for a ballerina, it must have been out of her reach to change the battery. He noticed this last night, and again while timing her shower this morning, she got in at twelve, and then out at twelve as well.

She did glance up at it, "About noon."

If he could leave all the little things she needs to stay herself now, he would. He would leave her impossibly perfect and unknown. He spent his college math classes studying time. He mostly just watched clocks, in an attempt to slow them down. He called it majoring in fingernail growth.

"Do you have work?" he asked.

"Nope," she said. "How old are you?"

He smiled. "Twenty-Two," he said. "I'm twenty-two."

He has a study group at two-thirty that afternoon.

She is suspicious though. Last night in bed below her breath, quietly, between moaning, she referred to him as her student. He did study her. She felt like a ballerina again, to be posed and pulled, tested and stretched. She did not feel old enough to be renewed. She is forty-two. She is the kind of woman that knows, really knows, how to do everything wrong, perfectly, the first time, no practice necessary, if she must. Last night he found her spine as perfectly fitted zippered teeth. From behind his thumb bounded the tip of each vertebrae as if neglecting gravity. He was skipping stones from one-second to the next, and his thumb moved as easy as time across her back.

"Well, let's just call this what it is."

Which was the loudest thing she had ever said, even after all the yelling in the bar the night before. She then motioned to the door, rushing him so much that upon leaving he continued to fail to find his shirt and just zipped his jacket up to his neck. He did so casually, it was all he felt he could afford, all that he had left. He thought to kiss her on his way out, but the strength with which she held the front and back of her door with her thumb and middle finger kept him from doing so.

. . . .

"Here's to us," was his first toast in the bar the night prior.

"Who are 'we' again?" was her response.

"Here's to never knowing what we will become, then," he said.

He thought about those quotes all day while walking home and stopped in several shops not far from her apartment. His father called to remind him of their plans for dinner for Mother's Day that night. He assured his father that he remembered, and noted that he was shopping for a gift as they spoke. He ended up buying his mother a small framed painting from an antique store he would not have visited if it was not for his one night stand with Hannah. The store clerk remarked on the painting's soft beautiful colors, "Shades of a sunset," he gestured. These coupled with the perfectly sharp cut angles of the frame reminded Jeff of Hannah as well as their night together. Jeff was never entirely sure whether he was paying more for the frame or the painting, he merely admired the symmetry of the situation.

. . . .

After he left she makes the bed, she fluffs the pillows and absentmindedly throws his lost sock and white shirt into her hamper. When she picks through her laundry she finds strands of hair, some blonde, some short, some long, some brown. She boils an egg and heats up some milk to add only a tablespoon of coffee to. She opens her computer to make sure she has recorded everything from the night before.

In the bar she made sure he would have to use the bathroom upon entering her apartment by urging him to finish his pint of beer quite quickly. She cited the city's lack of taxis as well as a falsifying rumor of an oncoming thunderstorm. It worked out well, as before asking for the all too common tour of her small apartment loft, he asked her where the toilet was.

While he was in the bathroom she checked the two microphones built into the headboard of her bed, then checked the two at either ends of the back posts. She checked the connection to her desktop computer, opened a program and clicked a red button labeled record. She then minimized the program and set a selected screensaver to blend in and out of the softest shades of a sunset, maintaining a certain kind of visual white noise.

In truth her clock only ever needed to read twelve. It was the time she needed the men she brought home to arrive, midnight, as well as the time for them to leave, noon. She wouldn't tell you it was broken, she would never admit to that, for her purposes it worked perfectly fine. Those were, after all, her work hours.

She ran through the recording with her eyes closed and placed herself back into the night. She cut and cropped the six or so hours of sleeping they did, leaving only his arrival, the sex, and the morning. She was hesitant about keeping the morning hours, and wondered why he had stayed. She took some notes regarding his appearance, actions, behavior and language on a word processing program then she dropped the audio file and the word processing file into a folder labeled "22" which corresponded with his age. She never recorded their names, for legal reasons, and always only took audio to protect their identity. The folder labeled 22 sat inside a folder labeled AudioPhile (the name of the project) along with other folders labeled the numbers between eighteen and forty-five. Not all twenty-seven folders existed just yet, but she hoped someday they would.

She would write a book about it, she thought, maybe a documentary would come to be. At least a study was being done.

. . . .

All day Jeff found his thoughts trailing back to Hannah's perfect bones. The small ones were necessary proponents to the large, his greater insignificant discoveries. He found himself wanting to go back and double check a few things, doubting himself, his eyes and hands, his imperfections. He missed a green light at a crosswalk trying to replace the symmetry and angles of her clavicles. It was interesting to him, to think of all the places she had been, rounding her off, all of her decisions, all of her lovers, always pushing her bones rounder. He decided to take some credit for this, he lent his pheromones to the last piece of her fitting puzzle. He blamed the trace calcium in the mudslide cocktail she stole sips from him at the bar. She stole them after making a comment regarding his inability to protect his chocolate milk in grade school.

After finally reaching his apartment he fished his best pants out of the back of his closet. He slid his arms down the sleeves of his father's college blazer, never purchasing his own, inheriting both the suit and the body to fit it. He would be late to his mother's dinner but only by ten minutes or so.

She spent her Sunday night running their night through various filters and scales that measured the tone, volume, and rhythm of the recording. She was searching for some sort of pattern, something she could measure, something that eroded over time. Their silence then became her downtime, until she came to measure and study it. She wanted to believe she was listening between the lines, waiting out for a whisper with a man at his most vulnerable. Sometimes she closed her eyes and thought she heard something universal, or consistent, between the recordings.

At dinner that night they separately wondered how many lovers it took to reach perfection, to find something together, selfishly.

Over the years he forgot her name, what avenue she lived off of, the day or even month of their encounter, but he remembered her perfect bones. He missed them enough. He vacationed on various coasts and islands, anywhere with a beach, if only to take in the sound of barefoot strangers walking silently along the sand. Again and again he found these trips to be a cheap disappointment. The waves only drowned out their silence. They still looked dead quiet, they looked perfect. To Hannah, Jeff remained nameless, his face and body blurred between files 23 and 21. The sounds of his love making forever documented in the darkness of an audio file. Their memories only truly kept what they were in the dark that night to begin with, ideas about bones and sounds. They were something worth studying, at the very least.

This is too much

"Do you want these clothes hangers?" She asked him.

In doing so she threw them directly onto the bed he'd claimed two hours prior. She claimed the down comforter and half the pillows. They lay neatly folded by her collection of mismatched though mostly blue and gold floral print luggage in the corner nearest the door, in the single room loft they rented for as long as a good real summer in San Francisco. By his count it was a strong solid five months, though her count was merely their three. The lease said four.

He noticed the four or five clothes hangers put to this test, should he protest, were all just wire. Ten minutes ago he watched from the corner of his eye as she stuffed all the thick white reliable hangers into her white trash bag. This heavy-duty-sixty-four-gallon plastic bag was all she had left to save her things with. He loved to see the plastic hangers shoved and showing like her thin bones through that bag. It reminded him of her ribs, hips, and oddly enough her tongue.

"No, you keep them. I know you have more clothes than me, keep them," he said.

He knew if that white plastic bag should burst, over weight under the one remaining street lamp lit on the corner of Folsom and Seventh, she might too. She might give, just give way to everything. The possibility of the white bag being abandoned due to unexpected breach excited him as well, in sympathy.

Then he thought of their pillows, he thought of the half he resigned to her. She fluffed them prior to her decision. She hugged and touched up all four of them, and then took the best. Of the even four pillows, two were introduced by each party upon moving in, then the various washing and buying of new matching cases misplaced their original owners identities entirely. Besides who honestly keeps in touch with their pillows among, amidst, a relationship? She swore she did, and he knew his interjections, most often over the smallest things, often led to violence. The larger discussions, however, were never violent for they most often occurred upon this couples intoxication, which weakened them greatly. It was better this way, he thought. These were the casualties of their love, his soft pillows and her wire hangers.

"Alright then," she said, "I'll take them. Anyway, you barely hang up anything anyway."

He just then noticed she used the word "any" way too much.

She grabbed the hangers and shoved them deep into the plastic bag, their ridges showing through. The white plastic of the bag going from two percent to skim in all of its most vulnerable places.

He smiled. He wondered. What else can I get into that bag?

I can drown you, he thought. I can break this.

Her mother sent her porcelain figurines in the mail every month. He despised them. They slowly assembled and assumed the entirety of their mantle, which he hoped would hold something with more character, such as the art of a friend, or an autographed baseball.

"I can't keep these," he said, "your mother would want you to have them."

They were ballerina cows in pink tutus, all shimmering in sharp leg kicks, their arms outwardly reaching. He helped her load them into her plastic bag, knowing the sharp edges and weight were working with him.

He wanted to give her his knives, yet he knew that he would miss cooking.

He wanted so badly for her hobbies to include bowling and for her to have a custom ball and for its case to go missing.

He wanted more weight.

He thought of their trip to IKEA months ago. He wished he would have thrown convenience to the wind. He wanted more awkward furniture to move. He knew once they brought it to this place, their place, together, it would remain, or it be a world-ending hassle to move out once again. He wanted that struggle.

Could awkward furniture be reason enough to stay together? He thought about the promises a couple makes when purchasing a full sized piano, or a billiards table. He thought about the sword in the stone. He moved on with her to the kitchen. Once there he helped her load her bag more, gave her half the forks and knives, then hid all the spoons.

She moved to the blender, "Don't you remember?" she asked him, "The blender was a gift from my father, it was a house warming gift to us."

"Oh yeah," he said. He thought of the last two words of her sentence, "To us."

He did remember. He remembered because the blender came with a note which she read out loud to him.

"This should help you blend in! With love, Dad." The note said. She read it in a high tone usually reserved for water cooler gossip mimicking over enthusiastic bosses among co-workers. This was a tone secretaries are born with, before they know they will become secretaries. A tone he experienced too much at his place of work, far far too much. So far too much, in fact, so much so, that he remembered reaching for the whiskey, the Coca-Cola, and a bag of ice to make them whiskey-coke slushies with their brand new blender right then and there, an action he remembered once interrupted by the blender's note.

Now though, months later, after their summer was over, she bent down to unplug the blender. "Wait," he stopped her, "I have an idea. Put down your trash bag, and wait a second." While opening the freezer door he said to her, "If you're going to take it, let's just, for one last time." He turned around with a bag of ice in his hand and forced a smile.

The sun was about to go down and that winter breeze that makes everyone's fingers a little more stiff blew in. Glove and scarf sales were on the rise, and he could think of nothing better than to make some blended drinks. She gave him a long lost look, somewhat confused, possibly irritated, ultimately questionable. Her silent protest for a speechless auctioneer. He turned up the heater, and then lit the fire place below the mantle where her figurines danced only twenty minutes ago. He closed the curtains and turned on the porch light in an effort to eclipse a false sense of daylight. He took off his coat then his sweater. He striped down to merely his jeans and a cotton t-shirt bearing a logo of a pizza shop in North Beach that he worked for in college. Returning to her he wished the hair on his forearms down. He wished the warmth back into their apartment, and faster.

"It's really starting to warm up out there. Are you sure you wouldn't like a frosty beverage?" he asked her, lying through his teeth.

He didn't wait for an answer. If this blender was partially his, in at least a time shared sense, it would be his right now. He reached for the whiskey, and when he did he reached for the highest bottle. It was by far out of her reach at the top of two

IKEA shelves they bought together, that he installed. Which he figured made them his, they were anchored to the wall with deep screws, and she didn't know how to use the power drill.

He poured in ice, then whiskey. Then he poured in the coke and then the last half scoop of vanilla ice cream he could find. He placed the lid back on the blender and held down the only button on the whole thing, simply labeled BLEND. It was loud, loud enough to drown her out like a good solid denial.

He grabbed their two favorite pint glasses. One with a large A on it, the other with a large matching T, which were their initials. He filled them to the top and handed her one, her head still slightly shaking in disagreement.

"To us," he said in cheers. He raised his glass and repeated the last two words she had said, "To us," he repeated them again, this time slightly smirking as the temperature in the room slowly began to climb.

"What do you make of all this?" she asked him, glancing around their loft after taking a shallow drink.

As she drank the possibility of pushing her limits continued to entertain him. It was, however, not the alcohol content, but her sensitivity for brain freeze that excited him. When she did encroach the ever paralyzing state of brain freeze, she did this incredible thing. She found the most bottom of her ears and pressed them with her thumbs. Then she let her forefingers rest with a slight pressure at the top of her ears and began to rub them in a timed sequence of five-seconds clockwise and five counter-clockwise. She did this with all of her free fingers reaching stretched outwards. Her eyes closed in all of this, possibly rolling around her head. The last piece, and what he wanted the most, was to know what became of her tongue in all of this.

He wanted her hands on her head making like a reindeer. He wanted her white plastic trash bag by her side bulging with perishables, the rising temperature causing the plastic of the bag to thin, to expand, to become weak.

They were an honest month before Christmas, he wanted this for Christmas, this weakness in all things.

"I don't know. Are we going out in style? I'm certainly having fun."

"That's not what I meant. Did you really think this would work out?" she again gestured about the messy loft.

He shrugged his shoulders.

By no means was this surprising for him. It became something of a necessity over the years, a tradition, no, an extradition. Since moving to San Francisco five years ago he spent every Christmas alone despite harboring girlfriends and affairs throughout the spring and summer. These were his marathons, and the line between training and running them had very much blurred. All he could ever always remember was lying on the floor coughing up liquor in his last mile, yet never finishing. At those times he couldn't ask more of his lungs than to cough, to throw themselves vigorously about his chest. For his throat to guide him to the success of becoming a marionette to the instinct of life.

This whole experience though, the closing of their accounts, it felt like that tour all renters take with their landlords after they give up their apartments. They admit to their hopeless defeats. Now he would have to find new excuses for the cigarette burns in the carpet. The unexplainable red stains in the bathtub. "She liked to color her hair," he thought he would one day say. "Except always, always red."

She did come to toast him, of course reluctantly. How else could she? She used her teeth as a thin grill to filter the chopped ice back into the glass, allowing only the whiskey and coke into her mouth. She had imperfect teeth now deemed perfect for this operation, and it made her smile when she thought of it.

"I'll only have this one," she assured him.

He held up the pitcher and pulled it off the blender's base then shook it to break off the ice that froze to the glass sides. "I suppose we'll have to finish this before we can clean it, otherwise, what a waste."

"That's perfect," she said, over thinking his statement, "we do have to finish this."

At this he finished his first glass and refilled it, leaving only a quarter of the blender still full. The blender came to four servings even, and the last bit was hers. He made it so by the loose gesture of waving it at her.

She left her stretched trash bag in the kitchen and wandered into their once bathroom. She didn't bother closing the door, and loudly played the cabinets and drawers, collecting forgotten hair dyes and shampoos. She trucked them back into the kitchen, dropping them in to the bag carelessly. She found her hair care product bottles to be shaped in such a way that the carrying of more than three was impossible. After the four required trips she rushed back with a box of Q-tips, the standard 500 pack. He smiled truthfully when he saw her confused face. He dreamt of them breaking it open and then splitting them clean even. Even if there was an odd number they could cut one in half. That was the beauty of Q-tips, every split couple was allotted their fair share. He knew she used them more often than him, but he didn't care.

"What about these then?"

He raced to a kitchen drawer and pulled a plastic sandwich bag out of a box, already half emptied ten minutes earlier.

"We can do this," he said.

He held the sandwich bag up like an answer. She once again gave him a confused look. He was far more intoxicated than she was, and she could tell.

"The box is yours, just give me half of what's inside." He said this nearly laughing, knowing the Q-tips would garner no weight nor pressure for her great bag of halves and must haves.

At this she laughed. It was a sarcastic, pitied laugh, "Really? Down to the last Q tip?"

"We can do this," he said again.

"Just have them, I can't do this, you maybe, but I can't."

She attempted to pick up her white bag yet its weight ultimately lead to her pulling and sliding it towards the door, the whole of it heavy and awkward. He thought to help her with it, but then came to realize if it should burst under his watch he may very well be blamed. It was after all full of smaller things, and his experience with smaller things was from time to time quite violent. The smalls of us we depend on to be large.

She trudged forward, her thin frame wearing about three outfits and now sweating from the heater and fireplace. These were the same three outfits she could not seem to fit into the suitcase that she had mentally labeled "clothes" earlier that morning as she began to pack to leave, without telling him, while he slept in, as he always did on Sundays. He woke that morning to her jumping and sitting on that same case once it was full, to get it to close. Brushing her bangs back behind her, she caught her breath and looked up at him, "A couple of months ago all my clothes fit in here," she said. A couple of months ago, she thought, I didn't have nearly as much of anything, this is too much.

"Where are you going?" he simply replied.

What You're Waiting For

I was in the shower measuring my pinkies when it happened. After five minutes of deliberation, it turns out they were deadlocked, but I wanted my left one to be stronger, thicker, and of better use. Throughout my entire life I played favorites, and today, inevitably, was the day of the pinkies. The water ran down in a manner all too casual and forgiving. I just ended a relationship a week prior and whenever the thought of her entered my mind, I proclaimed "to the shower and forever."

Besides, my fingernails always seem so much longer in the shower.

I could stand there all day and measure all of my lefts with my all of my rights, and I could play favorites, and mostly, be a little less than lonely. My stomach growled. It was two thirty in the afternoon, and I was becoming rather hungry. It was hard to think about food. I just woke up from a nasty hangover in an empty bed and said, "To the shower and forever."

It was a busy year. It was the same year I stopped blessing people after they sneezed, and it became long enough in that right alone. Winter finally came on like an exhale, a long moist one, after a year of sighing the months away.

The Consumer Electronics trade show back in June had finally belted out something that would change everything, these scientists finally figured it out. They could finally detect earthquakes. I always assumed that field of science to be dead and lost, that everyone in that big science building went down the hall to Cancer Studies or to Weapons Manufacturing.

What doesn't kill you?

It was slightly conversational and vaguely powerful.

These seismologists built this machine, and dropped it deep into the earth and let it tug and pull at all of our continental shelves. They did it with huge magnets, that were always either pushing or pulling, and we were always listening. It was like nagging your parents into spanking you. How much these devices caused or detected the earthquakes was unknown; we just had to know it was coming, even if we were the cause. Of course the first problem was due to the depth of these charges. The signal would take five to ten minutes to reach us, and at first everything would be five to ten minutes too late, telling us something we already knew. So they sped up the signal, and now everyone gets a warning of five to ten minutes prior to the earthquake. Everyone called that period of time "the window." Everyone asked what you did in the window yesterday, in that window, and everyone always remembered too.

Pacific Gas and Electric bought up all the shares and installed these radios into every household. They looked kind of like smoke detectors, and if you don't pay your utility bills on time they simply do not work. We were all afraid of not knowing, of the unknown.

It was either that, or you too can be alone in a city aware of an oncoming nightmare.

I was in the shower when it happened. The movie phone guy comes out full bore and starts yelling at me, he says, "There will be an earthquake in five to ten minutes!"

I had only just figured out the length of my pinkies, I was to the shower and forever. He was slightly conversational and vaguely powerful.

I thought to stay in the shower and let it go. The biggest fault of this new earthquake detection system was that there was no way of knowing if it was going to be a bump, a thud, or a thunderstorm. We knew something was wrong but we didn't know what, or to what degree.

I have a shower radio with a clock. I was hungry and I had five minutes to get out and get dressed and run straight into Golden Gate Park, which was a two minute jog or thirty-second sprint from my house.

I decided not to decide, my stomach still unkempt.

I found a vein, a thin blue one that ran up my left pinky finger, but with no twin vein for my right pinky. After carefully studying them for two minutes I came to the conclusion that we are not inkblots of symmetry. That scars, and well, life, saves us from our own identities, by identifying them.

"My pinky," I said to myself, "is my pinkies pinky."

Another big inhale.

And then I got to wonder if I was still drunk from last night, if this was a hangover, or if my teeth did hurt as often as they shouldn't.

And exhale.

"There will be an earthquake in the next two to seven minutes," blares the living room.

After that warning they will count down to the window, the five minutes of quiet when everyone waits, everyone either says "shhh" or "did you hear that?"

San Francisco was the first city to install these devices, and they backfired in the most peculiar way. These groups sprouted up, these earthquake fan clubs, bloggers and forums of people. When they first heard these alarms, first the five minute warning, then the declining others, they would run into their homes instead of out of them.

These people would run indoors in the five minutes and get into beds and get naked and fuck in the window. There were even retrofitted hotels that specialized in it, they rented by the window, and the waterbeds cost twenty dollars extra. That's what they called it, fucking in the window, for a whole new kind of thrill seeker.

I know because I was one of them. I work up the street on 9th Avenue waiting tables and so did my then future former girlfriend, except she was on 8th Avenue.

When the alarms came on, all our co-workers would run to that baseball field off Lincoln Way, and we would just sprint home. The adrenaline from the run and the countdown was the greatest aphrodisiac ever invented. It was like racing to get naked because you're skinny dipping in a spa in Alaska. Those earthquakes made the air still like Alaska.

Now she is gone, and I am alone in the shower with two minutes till the hiccup or the great collapse. I suppose I'll wait this out. I start to think of all the other people in this city in the shower when the alarm goes off. I am, I think, with them right now. I figure maybe I'm mostly alone. They are all running down staircases or falling down fire escapes, some of them naked, some of them wearing towels, mostly probably naked though.

There were these others too, this group that started up online. Some guy started it. He said when the alarm starts going off he's staying in, but he will have a light on that sits in his bay window, and if anyone wanted to join him for the big bump that they were welcome. He would have cookies and drinks and nobody should be alone in such a state of emergency. Of course, quite a few others followed, and it was a huge thing in the Castro.

In fact, an entire dating scene started with unlit lamps left in night windows. The lamps would be removed as soon as they were in a committed relationship, unless, they were into that kind of thing.

I have heard of webcam races to see who could build the biggest house of cards before the earthquakes hit. They built these indoors too, inside their very own house of cards. Somebody said it was a metaphor or something. The first alarm was the starting gun, and what a whistle it was. I saw a video of one once, this guy was sweating so much the cards stuck to his hands, then to themselves. All the judges ruled it cheating, and he was just crushed at the end. Figuratively crushed. It turned out that earthquake was just a baby tremor.

I did it too. After she left. I put a lamp out. The problem being, my window only faced my back yard, and it would only be visible from the courtyard of surrounding back yards. It was there though, and to be able to say that was enough, then to remove it someday was enough.

The wedding ring you take off when you get married.

It is nearly insane and impossible how impractically important these symbols became when we knew our world was about to shake and change.

To fall apart, to stay the same.

Yet, here I stand with one minute left, just staring at my toes. I know my shoes as well as the way I have walked for the last twenty-four years have pushed my toes into different directions. I know about the displacement of weight, weaker muscles due to vitamin deficiencies, shallow bones. All these factors adding up to the difference between the left and the right. I got to wondering if babies are completely symmetrical. They say that symmetry correlates rather closely to beauty, perhaps this is why babies are so cute, so beautiful.

I was once a baby too.

Alright, lets do this.

I don't dry off or put on socks. I don't grab my phone or my wallet. My jeans are half zipped, and my shirt is showing wet. When I'm running down the street the hard asphalt wears away at the tiny rings on my toes. As I chase crowds I can hear the birds sing, my hands in tight fists. On 8th Avenue I trip over an uneven slab of sidewalk and go down painfully fast and hard. I go down wrist and hand first, sliding into the sandpaper of the street. The alarms they placed on most all the city street corners are blaring all around me. The countdown is seconds from the five minute window, and I am a bleeding mess. I know now that shower got me so far away from anything soft, or safe, or clean.

By the time I get to the park, I can see all of them, all of the singles. They're milling about with cigarettes like they're waiting on test results. They stand around looking at their watches or phones, talking about the nothing before the big something. They scratch at their impatience with their new favorite fingernails. I swear it's a bar without any booze in that field. No one thought to bring a kite or a football, something to throw around while the big one finally hits. Then it occurs to me, this crowd would rather be with someone in danger than safe and alone. I can see their glazed-over eyes stare at a bright pink Victorian off 7th Avenue and Lincoln where strangers rush in with the same speed I had rushed out to the park.

I thought about safety.

I thought about hearing a tree fall in the woods and nobody believing you.

I have, however, come to find that my broken bloody hands and my pinkies for that matter look completely identical to each other after the fall. I can no longer play favorites. I have become a symmetrical inkblot, though a rather messy one. I feel born again. I fall back into the grass. The adrenaline coupled with my newly marred features leaving me a bit breathless dizzy. I have my ear to the ground, dirt on my cheek, listening to the angry belly of this earth. I can feel some ants, drawn to the sweet sugar of my blood, begin to congregate on my broken wrists.

The Burden of Legitimacy

At first there were footsteps, much like a metronome, a delicate kicking that measured at best my loss of rest. It felt much like sleeping on the sidewalk, with my ear to the ground, in the heartland of most all marching bands. Here they come again, count the time, creeping into my mind. I'm sure, it's probably just my mind.

This insomnia.

If you can't sleep and decide to write out the entirety of F. Scott Fitzgerald's The Great Gatsby on the top of your mattress you will surely wake up bruised in the impermanence of permanent markers.

If you are actually sleeping.

For I have learned and now must walk witness that the morning dew will wake the ink, before it will wake you.

It will wake you.

The book, those words, this ink, will transcend to your skin while you sleep, leaving you dressed in the last great American novel. It will be lifted and mirrored, bleeding and faded. In the morning sun, you eye a caterpillar ellipses that crawls up your arm. You wonder about a lonely question mark you found in the palm of your hand.

Good Morning.

The strangers you pass will stare and point at these new stains. They will not be regarded as the greatest achievements of the english language. They will scowl at your clothes, and your new temporary tattoos, you beauty-marked, type-writer-punched, drunk lover, you. That language, last nights dream, is now lost in the translation of your twelve-hour sleep cycle.

This is a dream.

The rewriting of great stories will not (as proposed) help you fill out your night. It will not help your insomnia or your bathing and grooming habits. You will breath in the chemicals that are produced purely to leave permanence, which are not so very good for your lungs or your skin.

You have taken in everything that does not matter.

I can tell you the best time to steal a good, clean, dirty, used mattresses is just after Christmas.

They are selling them for sleep.

I can tell you the best place to dump these mattresses after marking them up with your insomnia and novel dreams will never be a GoodWill store.

They are now worthless.

. . . .

Personally I have always found the trouble with stealing something profound, like a mattress, is the never quiet inside your head. Even when I'm stealing trash, I have this great never quiet, this static conscious. And it keeps me up.

Sometimes it's easy to forget why you're doing anything but continue without question to do it.

An addiction.

I don't know.

Have you ever dragged a duvet through Bay View? Halfway there, you get the feeling there might be a dead body wrapped up in it, maybe you forgot to check when you hurled it over your shoulder. So you check every two or three miles just in case. Have you ever practiced that first line to the cops, over and over again, you'll say to yourself, "It's just a duvet, it's just a duvet, it's just a duvet."

What are you afraid of?

Then someone hears you across the street, they just shake their head.

Congratulations.

Duvet.

. . . .

When I asked him how I should go about writing the next great American novel he said wait until it gets quiet, really quiet, then lie, very slowly, to everyone, about the swimming pool in the space station.

The what?

"The swimming pool in the space station."

Why won't you lie?

The Impossibilities.

Tell yourself something you don't know yet.

He told me the bible was the big bang, and every other piece of literature was a freckle on the face of a child in Arizona. Stranded thoughts from monkeys could be planets, no, no a lizards synapse could be a galaxy, but only if you agree with me, someday you too could be the last curve on a perfect circle.

They will lose you, and your little art too.

Religion makes the most sense in the desert, he said, he said they were so thirsty.

. . . .

It was Christmas Eve and I was dragging this twin Serta mattress down from Bernal Heights, hell I half rode the thing down some of those hills and this huge station wagon comes hauling right in my direction. I would say it was speeding easily fifty-five in a clearly marked thirty-five. Now, I've never driven a car, but I've heard them, all night.

It was a Volvo, this station wagon, which is Swedish for tank.

I'll say this again.

The trouble with the never quiet in my head is it sounds like Christmas morning. It sounds like ripping paper, screaming children, clapping, clapping, and clapping. Tonight it's even more so quiet now that the power lines have gone down. They may or may not be down because someones' neighbor's Volvo just careened into the transformer at the end of the street, and right when everyone's everything was almost asleep too, you should have heard it.

It was loud.

I have found that the never quiet is also how neighbors speak when they wish to sleep on this very special Christmas Eve. Tonight it sounds at best like a wide closed fist.

Welcome to my everything.

The explosion is rich and stirs the block. The lights flicker at the local hospital in the Labor Ward, and everyone says, "oh come on," or, "not again."

I see the lights on the whole block go out, and I imagine the children that thought to blame Santa for it. They hear their father falling down those dark stairs. He is making the sounds a jolly fat man is thought to make, though he's just fumbling for the flashlight they left in the drawer just to the right, no, no, to the left of the oven, where the cookies never finished baking.

It's a beautiful sight if you ever have the chance to see it, the force of an old unstoppable Volvo rushing head first into an immoveable transformer box. It was his stop.

The big bang before the ever-expanding quiet.

Those sparks though, they are something I have known; they were old fireflies in Mississippi.

I was walking home and the poor Volvo swerved to miss me, wearing a mattress like an angel target on Christmas Eve. For the first time the weight wasn't what nearly killed me. This was of course days after what I was entitled to finishing. Tonight I was merely running an errand for a friend who desperately needed a place to sleep. I was just finishing up some last minute Christmas shopping.

. . . .

About a week earlier I was crashing in a dumpster at the mattress factory out in Bay View.

It was my home.

I went straight to the source like they had asked me. When I could, I slept in it like I had the world beat. Everything was soft and white and clean, though it still felt a close second to Mississippi.

"Moving to Mississippi was easy, but when the cops asked me to spell it backwards as proof of my residency, well I lost my count and moved back to San Francisco," I told Jay.

"Mississippi is the cotton capital of the United States," I said, softly.

I met Jay on a loading dock, while I was collecting mattresses, collecting and discarding. He was tall and thin with arms that swayed in the two count of time, his facial hair curled as soon as it could, with a beard built on bedsprings that helped him sleep.

Jay has never been to Mississippi, but he seemed to get behind what I was after, what I wanted to do, my grand scheme.

Hell I even asked him how many words those Eskimos had for snow, while we were freezing nonetheless, and he just looks at me, and he says, "Enough."

He starts rolling a cigarette with half tobacco and half chamomile, his fingers busy typewriter rollers crushing then feeding the paper in and out of his folded praying hands. He places the cigarette between his thin lips into his small mouth enveloped by his huge beard; it's a goddamn match in a haystack.

Jay is always out to cure my insomnia, though never conventionally.

"Three hundred years ago up on Russian Hill," he tells me, "these peaceful tribes would gather for multiple weddings, but they didn't call them weddings… And they would drape their brides in chamomile and jasmine, they would burn sage, and the bay winds would blow through forcing everyone to inhale all these relaxing things, I think Rosemary too. And with great sighs, these strangers, they would get as high as love and laughter, they would gather and they would say, 'what a beautiful day.' Everyone would say it in some dead language."

"Why don't you smoke Jasmine as well?" I asked.

"It's much better as a tea or incense. Besides, I could never smoke something with such a beautiful name."

"Did you know…"

'Did you know' are Jay's three favorite words.

"Did you know the first radio only had one station, one microphone and one receiver but they didn't call it a radio, they called it a telephone?"

"Don't you mean Morse code?"

"No, that's like saying the first language was a language at all, or the first human was a person."

"I see," I say, and I'm okay with Jay being right, I'm perfectly square with Jay being wrong. I've known him nine days and I am beginning to know more about nothing than I will ever.

"Today, Jay, I need you to go down to the old tracks by the CalTrain station, China Basin, collect railroad spikes, collect not steal, the difference is up to you."

"I'm going down to the packing yards to collect, not steal, the thickest zip ties."

We were off, except not, because luck would have it after saying our goodbyes, we ended up walking in the same direction for about ten blocks which is when I got a couple more, "Did you knows."

"You know the difference between a flute player and a snake charmer?"

"What, Jay?"

"Fear."

"Did you know Egyptians invented the pyramid scheme?"

We stopped at a construction site and he pointed down at some wet cement, "I love this stuff, have you ever been published?" he said.

"No, Jay."

He grabbed my finger and I nearly fell in. On my knees I wrote, "Permanence is nothing unless spelled correctly." I wrote it because I knew Jay would like it, what a kick. It was my way of saying, "Did you know?"

"Did you spell it correctly?"

"I'm not so sure." I replied.

. . . .

I want to force railroad spikes through mattresses and in doing so thread them with zip ties and bind them like books. I don't want to use nylon or bungee cords, I want it to look clean, thick, one book per mattress with thinner ink. Like a spring loaded sandwich, and we can climb in and read and sleep. I'll write out all the classics. I nearly have them memorized. I do, and I write them out when I can't sleep. Then I want to write out my own story on the back of the last mattress. I write it with a pen name like Alfred Chinsky or William Butterfield, maybe even Henry Ryan Catcher. Why do they always have those names, those huge names? Then I'll leave the whole damn thing on the doorstep of the Museum of Modern Art. They will examine the easy metaphor, those prim art professors, those staunch noses inhaling the ink like bitter coffee stink. "It's a story as a soft place to hide, a warm place to sleep, It can easily hide one or two bodies, as most great November novels do," they will surely say.

Yes, yes, yes.

They can go on about it, those professors, pay no one, call it street art, maybe it will unfurl like a flower, maybe it doesn't need to, maybe I can just hide in it, hide in it and sleep.

. . . .

Upon my return to the dumpsters of the mattress factory I find Jay with some old man all wrapped up in a sleeping bag. He must have won that potato sack race in fourth grade, I think. His father must never look at him the same, I figure, I joke, I kid to myself.

Though as I'm walking up, Jay tells me I'll love this one, that he was once the heir to some Tampon fortune. Given the circumstances and where the money came from he didn't know where to put it. So in jest, and as he does so well, he called himself a romantic, and he put it back into women. He tells me he donated the millions to breast cancer research. The whole thing was a firework for a sinking ship in the Atlantic, or maybe it was just a sonogram on the right Sunday for a nun, it doesn't matter, he tells me, because it wasn't his money anyway.

Thanks Jay.

The sleeping bag man's name is Bryce. He introduced himself in all the most polite and peculiar ways. Bryce has long thin brown hair that sways as he walks and when he sneezes, which he often does, it kicks up like a horses mane, then it stays whichever way it lands until the next sneeze. He tells me he has trouble keeping anything the same.

Bryce helped Jay collect railroad ties, Bryce tells me he doesn't believe in crucifixion though he very much enjoys the use of x in such a violent word.

Then he tells me Religion makes the most sense in the desert, they were so thirsty, are you thirsty?

I tell him, I, we, won't be crucifying anyone, but books, I guess, or maybe just mattresses, I suppose, and I thank him. He asked me if he could borrow one of my mattresses for the night, "Before I string it up," he says, and I said, "sure, stay awhile."

Bryce, Jay and I stay up all night talking crazy wrong about everything, the moon above us pressing its skull into the night. For a couple hours we couldn't see a thing except the moon and our cigarette cherries, our old fireflies. Then we turned old lampshades upside down. Bryce says he once wore them as hats. We turned them upside down and lit small fires inside them, until they burned out like tight open fists, like little things trying to keep the fire in. When all we had left were copper wire brace bones, we built frames for the next half hours' lampshade. I can tell you ten lampshades will last you five hours and it looks good enough to dance to, to sing to, and to talk about. The canvases of these lampshades burn yellow then brown, then the thin ash of waste.

We talked all night like you do when you're a kid in, or on, a bunk bed. I was always on the bottom looking up. So we talked like kids not ready to go to bed. Jay tells me he spent years down at the docks putting rubber bands on lobster claws, and I knew someone did that too, that's what I told him. Bryce tells me he invented the miniature umbrella they put in all those tropical drinks, but no one would buy the idea because it never rains in the tropics. Now Bryce hates the tropics, curls up into a sleeping bag and just hides. He tells me the worst day wasn't when he found out that idea had made millions, the worst day was when he was served a Pina Colada in Seattle on a rainy day, like pouring rain, and they gave him a business version of the miniature umbrella, one with a curved cane at the end and a black tarp roof of a skin. "It hurt to see his baby with a bastard son," was how I remember him putting it. So he says he moved to San Francisco for the fog, that the sun and the rain had both shamed him.

After they both talk themselves to sleep, they start snoring something loud and choking, so I dragged my mattress out of the triangle we formed with the fire in the middle. I dragged it over to a two-foot concrete wheelchair accessible ramp and tried my best to sleep slightly propped up. You can see the stars in Bay View, don't let anyone tell you otherwise. Out by the old shipbuilding yards you can stare across at Oakland and skip stones across the water with hopes they will make it back to someone else's dry land. I wanted to roll over and start writing out Ulysses or The Picture of Dorian Gray on my bed. It's a nervous hand and pinball head I've got, but I know it will just smear the moisture when the morning comes.

I have to piss so I head over to the row of porta-johns at the construction site next to the mattress factory.

When I arrive, I must admit drunk myself, it continues to be these cave painting scrawls, these silliest of truths written on these bathroom walls that amuse me.

"If you know me, you don't know me, here."

"The following statement is true... The previous statement is false."

"Moses was wrong there's sand everywhere."

"I'm sorry."

"If your name is Jasmine my number is 7143570619 if it isn't, it isn't."

. . . .

The next morning I send Bryce and Jay off to find two PVC pipes about three feet long with a one and a half inch diameter. I need one for an air reservoir and one for the barrel. I also told them to pick up as many valves, elbows and connectors as they could find.

I need a propulsion system of some sort, preferably an air tank and some new thicker, stronger, staying ink, something that will set in old cotton and evade the elements.

"Why are you doing all this? Is it because you can't sleep?" Jay asks, once again rolling a cigarette, this time with the contents of an Earl Grey tea bag. I can see his eyes darting back and forth between his automatic hands armed with meticulous fingers.

"Why do anything?" I tell him with a conviction to apathy, which I am sure does not exist. "They say if you play back the sounds of crickets chirping to the same original crickets they will react as if threatened by the sounds of themselves, they also say that a dog will play with its reflection for hours."

"So you're playing with your own reflection or you're threatened by your sounds? And who are 'they'?"

He's not getting this.

"No, no, everyone else is afraid. This, this is a picture that keeps the dog's attention, this is the sound that keeps the crickets quiet."

I can tell you what I mean. I can say this to Jay, and it does not matter. When I started this I had to be crazy, looped, lost on one end. I was homeless, alone, nomadic, up all night listening to crickets, but I had to finish it so it could make sense to me. We can't see the light when we run under Buena Vista Park through the sunset tunnel, but we keep running, we do stupid things, and sometimes it feels triumphant.

I had to make sure that I was not going through the motions and that the motions were going through me.

And yes it was, in part, so that I could sleep.

Jay and Bryce are walking down the hill. I can hear them muttering strange words like vacuum and hypocrisy. I am, however, not worried. Thanks to my odd and simple pleas of nonsense talk I have negotiated yet another day of free labor.

I headed back out to Hunters Point to collect an air tank, which was not very difficult to find, thanks to the beautifully abandoned and plentiful shipbuilding graveyards that turned into junkyards after the 1950s. I found a toaster on my way and spit into the glaring aluminum panel. After rubbing and shining it with my jacket sleeve I caught my reflection. I haven't seen my face in weeks and my eyes, from what I can see, are beat red and plump. My face is sun burnt dried blood red. I had no idea. It never hurt from the lack of sleep. Nothing hurts, it just gets worse. The pain is always awake. With one look at my face I wonder if Jay and Bryce aren't doing this entirely out of pity.

After about an hour of digging around, I spotted it. My source of pressure, an air tank, and it was drowning in a sea of waste. The luck in finding these obscure items sometimes feels as if they were meant for this project. They were meant to shoot threaded railroad ties through mattresses with Lolita and Brave New World hand written on them. Sometimes I can convince myself of anything at all.

Absolution.

I've read all about potato cannons that kids are building for their high school science fairs. They ended up keeping the B+

grade and the felony charges for destruction of property. This was the atom bomb in the hands of an estimate, the learning curve sloping downhill into the dangerous territory of boredom and insomnia. Down at the local library I studied diagrams and printed out blueprints for these cannons with the age-old excuse of building something for its proper use.

After procuring my two-foot tall by two-feet around air tank, I took the 30 Stockton bus to a florist on Third Street. Here I had to reassure them that the tank was not stolen, that we all had a right to air, that it was quite possibly the last expense of life we shall never pay for. I said all of this while taking a very deep breath.

He gave in after I promised him the tank once I was done with it. I left him with my one and only twenty-dollar bill to keep good on that promise. I kept that twenty for only one reason, collateral. No one likes to be used, but everyone needs to. I'm just hoping I have the pressure to put these railroad spikes through cotton and springs, without making a mess of everything.

I beat Jay and Bryce back to the loading docks and started sharpening the railroad spikes on various surfaces around the area. Though one was all that was necessary, I told them to gather quite a few spikes so as to procure the sharpest and least rusted of the bunch. The spikes commonly used in San Francisco during the gold rush were cast iron. I needed something harder, like steel, and I needed it sharp.

Behind the loading dock of a nearby abandoned warehouse I found a wrecked, worn, painfully large and heavy stainless steel tire rim that I am assuming once belonged to a dump truck. I wondered about the abandoned warehouse. Was it a chop shop that was ironically sold? It appeared parted out, like its intentions, like a butcher gone hungry.

After rolling the rim back to the mattress factory I ran a steel pole through where the lug nuts go. Then I slid the pole between the open slats of some wooden pallets. This left the rim hanging inches from the ground yet free spinning. I licked my lips while spinning the wheel freely with my hand. I then connected the long end of the steel pole that shot out of the other end of the wooden pallets to the rear axel of a child's bike that Jay had been riding all day.

"It's okay, I'll give it back," I assured him.

Then with the removal of the bicycle's front wheel the front end rested on the forks. It propped itself up at an angle of no more than forty-five degrees leaving the back wheel lifted off the ground. We then spun the seat around to face the raised back end and made a human-powered sharpening wheel.

Jay didn't mind pedaling as I worked the spike against the inside of the spinning rim. I think it's because he liked to see the sparks. I did too, we called them fireflies.

Without goggles I became entranced with the red hot spike licking the spinning rim on the cold night. The golden rain of warmth found and stung my hidden naked skin where it could, in a small hole in my jeans, a fingernail here, and my lips through the ski mask I wore for protection. I showered in the sparks and when they caught me I took the sting, like a beekeeper. I was a beekeeper, and I was here for the honey. I wanted nothing more than to beat the red-hot tip of the railroad spike with a hammer. I wanted to be a blacksmith, a beekeeping blacksmith in a mattress sewing circle.

I thought about how these railroad spikes held the country together by stapling it shut, man made roads for robot trains. Then, when they were pulled, like stitches from the sky, the scars kept. Those borders, after all, tell us where we live. Everything is squares from the sky, quilted for your convenience.

The Midwest's fields of grain tickling your nose as you sleep in the quilt of the country. I think right around then is when Jay says I lost my balance, fell forward and nearly killed myself, passing out face-first, inches from the red hot spinning steel rim. He said I slept well though, was out the whole night, like a baby below a furnace.

. . . .

I woke up to find the railroad spike sharp enough to harpoon a whale, a big white one if necessary. Without waking the others I went ahead and assembled my pressurized cannon exactly how the blue prints explained. I felt like a kid on Christmas morning, opening my gifts without anyone the wiser.

Jay woke up to the whistle of the air tank as I tested the strength of the PVC pipe. It was perfect. "Is it ready yet?" he asked.

"Nearly, do you have the time?"

"Oh, no, I don't, I gave up."

"You gave up?"

"Every watch I've ever owned fell slow, so about a year ago I gave up."

He tells me this as he rolls a cigarette, this one with peppermint and tobacco, I suppose the purpose being to freshen up his morning breath.

"Hey Bryce," I yell, "do you have the time?"

Bryce doesn't hear me. Bryce is reading the Sunday Funnies, he doesn't even look up, lost in it.

"Well, I give up too," I tell Jay. "Let's give this a test."

I shaved the T on the end of the spike into a perfect circle this morning and as expected it fits perfectly into the barrel of the gun. I fed the spike down the throat of the barrel with the bare end of a broom; I needed it tight and taut.

Since any sort of written documentation felt slow and cumbersome I merely announced to my compatriots the plan of attack I would be following.

"Test run number one: Railroad spike without zip tie to be fired at fifteen PSI into top right corner of test mattress one… also known as Bryce's bed."

I swear I can see Bryce's ears breach from underneath his long thin hair.

I turn the red knob on the air tank to the left and listen to it whistle till the gauge reads fifteen, then spin the knob back to the right to cut the flow. Then yank the first lever up to lock the pressure within the reservoir, then the second lever down to let it release the other end. It's all red-light, green-light with the spike waiting on the throw. It's loud not like an accident, it's loud like a bullet, like a purpose, like a vehicle.

"Result: No leaks found in the piping, spike penetrated six inches of mattress yet failed to make a clean pass through." I documented loudly. "Test run number two: Railroad spike unthreaded to be fired at thirty PSI into bottom left corner of Bryce's mattress."

We ran the same procedure except this time I let Jay throw the final switch and it's twice as loud, it's a goddamn train through a tunnel.

"Result: No leaks found in piping, Spike clearly passes through mattress devoid of any springs within its path."

"Ah come on guys," Bryce's Sunday funnies taken seriously suddenly seem much less innocuous, "I really liked sleeping on that."

Bryce knows about my insomnia. I think that he thinks I'm just taking revenge on those that keep me awake. Taking life out on soft things, breaking everything on me.

"I'm telling you I only shot it through the corners, and only twice. We should be celebrating. It works. I half expected something to go wrong, something always goes wrong."

Jay and I threaded up the spike for the first official pass through the first official mattress, which was to be the cover of the book of books made of mattresses.

And success.

We found the greatest strategy was to navigate just to the left of the first row of springs, pull the lever and start punching holes in it. The book was to be a total of five mattress that when stood up and viewed from the sky made a sort of five pointed snowflake or star. I chose to write out the first of the ten novels on the front cover. The last story, the one on the back cover would be mine.

I pinched these mattresses together one after the other; the noise was nothing new, like a staple gun reintroducing the splits into my scalp, it felt like my dreams, when at least I thought I was sleeping.

I wasn't.

I was rewriting the second book by my new favorite author.

I was writing out Catch-22 and Darkness At Noon, I was putting these things to rest, into mattresses, into beds, where the nightmares go.

This could be a journal or an epitaph.

A used mattress gains up to twenty pounds of dead skin, oh the weight. A book gains a quarter ounce of dead skin if it is lucky, some old relic bibles about a half an ounce of person. A half an ounce of person has been left in a book.

Dead skin.

I myself have woken with a tenth of an ounce of ink, in the form of a book, most likely a classic, all over my skin. The wrinkles outside my eyes folded into pages painted with the thoughts of men and women before me who also could not sleep. A tenth of an ounce of a book left on a person.

Dead ink.

By the time I finished, Bryce was sleeping in the big blue dumpster that housed me these first few weeks. Jay was out like his dreams on a pile of cardboard atop the wooden pylons, tossing and turning and rediscovering things. I found them both asleep at best uncomfortably. I started a fire next to our old lampshades and boiled some water for tea. Knowing that Jay would only smoke it, I only made half of a pot for Bryce and I.

I envy them, and I know about eyes and exercise and patience. All of the blind play music in their minds, and the deaf sleep in flowerbeds to wake up next to the sound of seeing something beautiful. They live at the edge of anything, with a heightened sense of being exempt, and they never need justification. Well, leave me in my mattress sandwich. Let's pretend, lets just pretend. I can see forever, and I can hear forever, with no rest.

While rewriting my novel for the last time, the one on the back mattress cover, the seven blisters still left on my three favorite knuckles popped. They were on my left hand, the one I write with. They popped and stained the mattress with the same decency as a lover that doesn't know how to stop, keep going, keep going. We are almost there, and then we sleep.

This is a run on sentence, this insomnia.

But I'm sick of it.

Tomorrow I'm headed up to Bernal Heights to pick up a Duvet for Bryce and a twin Serta for Jay, I told them they would be rewarded for their help. Besides tomorrow night is Christmas Eve, and they are good people.

www.ingramcontent.com/pod-product-compliance
Lightning Source LLC
Chambersburg PA
CBHW060045150626
46556CB00018BA/2704